This book belongs to

Published 2021 by Macmillan Children's Books
an imprint of Pan Macmillan
The Smithson, 6 Briset Street, London EC1M 5NR
EU representative: Macmillan Publishers Ireland Limited,
Mallard Lodge, Lansdowne Village, Dublin 4
Associated companies throughout the world
www.panmacmillan.com

ISBN 978-1-5290-7066-8

1 3 5 7 9 8 6 4 2

A CIP catalogue record for this book is available from the British Library.

Printed and bound by CPI Group (UK) Ltd, Croydon CR0 4YY
Designed by Suzanne Cooper

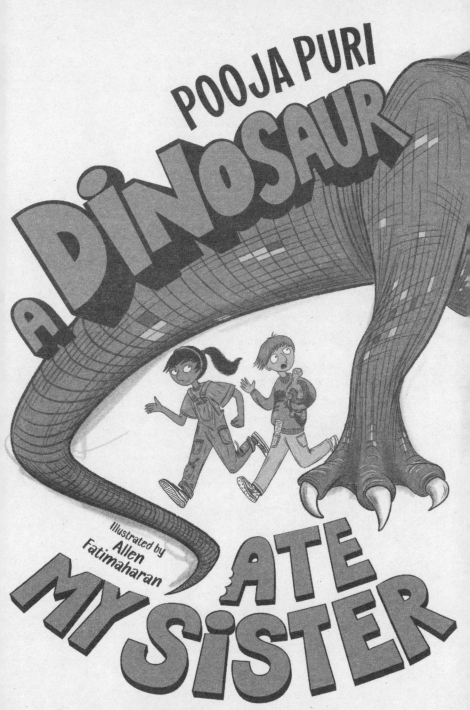

POOJA PURI

A DINOSAUR ATE MY SISTER

Illustrated by
Allen Fatimaharan

MACMILLAN CHILDREN'S BOOKS

For my family –
thanks for everything.
P. P.

Welcome to my Book Club

I'm so excited that you are able to join us. I hope you have a smile on your face today.

The first book I've chosen for you is *A Dinosaur Ate My Sister*. It's the perfect story to escape into, to find adventure and to inspire you to follow your dreams.

I want you to take this book home tonight and write your name in the front because it belongs to you and only you (it's obviously fine to share with friends and siblings but only if YOU want to). Tell your friends that this book was chosen by me for you.

If you're struggling, don't be afraid to ask for help. We all need help along the way - me included. There is no rush to get to the end. Enjoy every word at your own pace. I'm so excited to hear what you think.

Get that head of yours high and let's conquer the day together.

With love,

MR

Note From The Author

Before you start reading, there are a few things you should know:

1. I, Esha Verma, am a **genius inventor extraordinaire**.
2. There is nothing I cannot invent. This includes words.
3. I like lists.
4. I did not mean to send my sister back to the Age of the Dinosaurs. That was HER OWN FAULT (Mum and Dad, if you're reading this, please take note).
5. This book is a journal of my adventures. Technically, it is a journal of my ADVENTIONING (my inventioning and the adventures that come after).
6. This book should have been called *The Long and Terribly Twisted Stories of Time Travel, Dinosaurs and Other Things That Happened as Told by a Genius Inventor Extraordinaire*. My apprentice, Broccoli, promises he wrote the title correctly, but it mysteriously changed without his knowledge. I told him there is nothing mysterious about it and that he shouldn't have let his tortoise, Archibald,

anywhere near this journal. If I still had ~~my~~ our time machine, I could have fixed that. Of course, if I had a better apprentice, it wouldn't have happened at all.

[A note from Broccoli: Archibald had nothing to do with it. Esha is just cross because we don't have our time machine any more.]

[Another note from Broccoli: I am an excellent apprentice.]

A Second Very Important Note From The Author

No dinosaurs were harmed in the writing of this book.

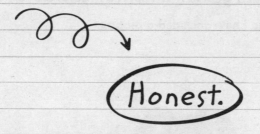

Honest.

A Third Even More Important Note From The Author

I am sure that you, the Reader, are foot-hoppingly desperate to know what a **genius inventor extraordinaire** looks like, so I have included a picture:

The Brain Trophy

This is the Brain Trophy.

Beautiful, isn't it? There is only **ONE** Brain Trophy in all of existence. Each year, at a special ceremony, it is given to the **BEST** Young Inventor of the Year.

Winning the Brain Trophy is:

① Extremely difficult (even more difficult than jellybean juggling or sneezing with your eyes open).

② Like walking on the moon — only **BETTER**.

③ My dream of ☆DREAMS. ✦ ☆

You probably can't tell from the picture, but the Brain Trophy is made from the coolest and rarest rock **EVER**: ZIRBOONIUM. You might think that a lump of rock doesn't sound very cool, but you'd be wrong. Wrong and wrong. Double wrong. A DRONG just like my big sister, Nishi. ~~If you've picked up this book, then you're probably not a drong . . . well, I hope you're not. But if you think there is even the tiniest chance that you *might* be a drong you can put down this journal right now and look for something less exciting to read like—~~

As I'm absolutely sure you're <u>not</u> a DRONG, I can tell you that:

① Zirboonium was found in a meteorite which fell to Earth from space. This means it is **NOT OF THIS WORLD**.

② Nobody really knows where zirboonium is from. This means it is an **UNKNOWN** substance.

For inventors, **UNKNOWING** is one of the best things in the world. Unknowing gives you tickles in your toes, itches in your britches and makes you feel spine-tingly all over. Unknowing is where inventioning begins. That's why all the ultra-**genius** people of the world decided to turn the zirboonium meteorite into a trophy:

THE Brain Trophy.

To enter, contestants have to be between 7–16 years old. The winner is invited to visit the top-secret headquarters of Genius & Extraordinary Inventions Inc (aka **GENIE**) before going on a special tour to show their mind-boggling, prize-winning invention **ALL OVER THE WORLD**. Their name is carved on the Brain Trophy with a super-sharp laser pen and they become an inventor legend for all eternity. All the greatest inventor legends are on it; Einstein won it when he was 8 years old (the youngest **EVER**), Nancy Johnson won when she was 10 and Alexander Graham Bell and Grace Hopper both won when they were 12!

From the moment I was old enough to enter the contest, I've had a space ready for the trophy on my table – right next to my extremely valuable first edition *Inventor's Handbook*, my complete card collection of Genius Inventors through History and my Inventor's Thinking Hat (which I invented myself – obviously).

When I am inventioning, the Brain Trophy is all I can think about. If I close my eyes, I can see my name on it next to all the great **geniuses** of this world and I feel so spingly **that I think**

I might **explode.**

(and a few other things ...)

At first, everyone was really excited about me being an inventor.

'The right invention could make us rich enough to buy a football team,' said Dad. 'It's all a question of probabilities.' (He is a Maths teacher.)

'The right invention could make us rich enough to buy a football team *each*,' said Mum, picking up the phone. 'Hello, Aunty Usha. Yes, I'm quite sure it's not bunions.' (She is a *podiatrist* and Aunty Usha's favourite niece.)

'Thar rit invenshun coo ba me a noo set of teesh,' grinned Dadaji.

'Or the iPhone 100,' said my cousins, Mina and Bina.

'Ice-cream!' said Arjun. He was three.

That was a few years ago.

Now, I think everyone is tired of waiting to become millionaires. Especially Mum and Dad. 'If you spent as much time on your schoolwork as you do inventing, Esha Verma,' says Mum, 'we wouldn't have to keep apologizing to the neighbours about the explosions and the smoke and the weird smells!'

So much for perseverance.

Nishi thinks I'm wasting my time. 'You don't really think inventors exist now, do you? Everything you could ever invent has already been invented.' Which just shows what her brain is filled with (clue: DRONGNESS).

The only person that really understands the importance of inventioning is my apprentice, **Broccoli**.

What
I actually
look like

I guess I should probably tell you about him.

Ten Important Things You Should Know About Broccoli:

① Broccoli's dad fixes telephone lines and his mum fixes people's teeth. They are both very quiet and sensible. They talk about quiet, sensible things in quiet, sensible voices. They are not like my family. AT ALL.

② Broccoli is *exactly* like his mum and dad.

③ When Broccoli gets scared, he sneezes. He sneezes so often that he has a permanent trail of broccoli-shaped snot dangling from his nose. It looks a bit like this:

1. Definitely Dangling Drip: tiny bit scared

2. Dangerously Dangling Drip: a bit more scared

3. Get-a-Tissue Drip: extremely scared

4. Nuclear Nose Drip: full fright mode aka panic stations

④ Broccoli's real name is James Bertha Darwin. He is the grand-son of the famously fearless fossil hunter, **Brave Bertha**. Unlike his grandmother, Broccoli is not brave *or* fearless.

⑤ Broccoli is **boggly** about dinosaurs.

⑥ Last month, Broccoli's grandmother Brave Bertha discovered a fossil of an **UNKNOWN** dinosaur. The Fossil Federation was so excited that they named the dinosaur the Berthasaurus. When Broccoli saw his granny on the front cover of *Dinosaur World*, he burst into tears (the happy kind).

⑦ Broccoli's grandmother sends him the **BEST** presents. Not boring granny presents like tea sets or perfumed tissues. Dangerous, ferocious presents that p^{o}p and snap and **EXPLODE** without warning. Broccoli is scared of most things, but he loves his grandmother, so he always keeps what she sends him.

⑧ The ~~evillest, worst~~, most *interesting* present that Broccoli's grandmother ever brought him is Archibald. Archibald is the son of Archimedes, Bertha's own tortoise. Like his pa, Archibald is always ready for adventure.

Archimedes

Archibald

What Archibald
actually looks like

⑨ The last present that Broccoli got through the post was
a Screeching Fizzer Firecracker from somewhere deep in
Japan. The Screeching Fizzer Firecracker is so loud that it's
banned in twenty countries. Broccoli is so afraid of Archibald
accidentally eating/stealing/flying away on it that he always
carries it around in his pocket. [It would be helpful to
you, the Reader, to remember this for later in the story.]

⑩ Broccoli does not always say very much. This is another
reason he is (mostly) a good apprentice.

[A note from Broccoli: I don't say very much because I don't usually
get the chance.]

You might wonder why a super-duper inventor like
me needs a snot-nosed apprentice. The truth is that an
apprentice comes in very handy for doing all the things
that an inventor is simply too busy to do, like hoovering the

carpet (inventioning is a messy job), buying fizzpops when you're grounded (which is most of the time) and taking notes about **grand ideas** (when your brain is bursting with so much **genius** it's hard to keep track). In fact, apprentices are so useful that I wonder why everybody doesn't have one. Together, we are

☆ THE ☆
TEAM
OF
☆ DREAMS. ☆

In the last three years, Broccoli and I have entered a grand total of **three** inventions into the Young Inventor of the Year contest:

INVENTION 1: THE **EXTEND-A-HAND**

Result: 2nd place.

To give a helping hand for when you're just too busy. Suitable for multiple functions including long-distance throwing, nose-picking, remote-control-lifting, bum-scratching, tortoise-rescuing.

INVENTION 2: SELF-CLEANING SPECS

Result: 2nd place.

Designed for ALL weather conditions, including blizzards, cyclones, hurricanes and sandstorms.

INVENTION 3: INSTA DE-STICKER SPRAY

Result: 2nd place.

Guaranteed to help you out of every sticky situation.

We're the only inventors in the contest's history to have come second place three times in a row. I checked. But not this year. This year I was absolutely 100% certain that we were going to win the Brain Trophy. Because this year we'd invented something to blow the judges' socks off. Something so brilliant that it would make their hair stand on end and their eyeballs pop out of their sockets at the same time.

This year, we'd invented a

time machine.

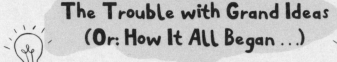

The Trouble with Grand Ideas
(Or: How It All Began ...)

The *Inventor's Handbook* says that all great inventions start off as a grand idea. The trouble with **grand ideas** is that they are one in a gazillion. Which is why, eight weeks before the next Young Inventor of the Year contest, I called a Brain-sparking Meeting with Broccoli at Inventor's HQ ... aka my room.

'What we need,' I told him, 'is to think outside the box. What we need is an idea that's so spingly, so amazing, that the judges have to give me – I mean, us – first place. Last year, we were beaten by an AUTO-DRYING TOWEL. Are you making a note of this?'

Broccoli sniffed and continued scribbling furiously in his notebook. He was perched on the end of my bed with Archibald pretending to be asleep beside him.

It was part of our Apprentice–Inventor Agreement that Broccoli would take notes of all our Brain-sparking Meetings for future reference. I gave him a notebook especially. After all, when I'm a famous millionaire inventor, I'm absolutely sure people will want to read my very important thoughts.

'What we need,' I said, 'is to think of a **GRAND IDEA**. The question is: **how?**'

Broccoli took an extra-enormous sniff. Next to him, Archibald was sneakily examining the distance between my bed and the open window.

'Well, how did you come up with your other **grand ideas?**' asked an unsuspecting Broccoli.

'Moments of brilliance,' I said, and shut the window. Archibald gave me a villainous glare that I ignored. 'But it's hard to be brilliant all the time.'

'Why don't you check the *Inventor's Handbook*?' he said without looking up from his notebook.

For an apprentice, this was not a bad idea. In fact, it was a very good idea. Maybe some of my **genius** had started to rub off on him.

I turned to the back of the *Inventor's Handbook* and ran my finger over the index until I found what I was looking for.

'Here it is,' I said. 'Inventor's Block. Page four hundred and twenty.'

I turned to the middle of the book and read aloud. '*Stuck in a rut or unsure of what your next big invention should be? Suffering from the effects of a not-so-successful idea? You are not alone! Every genius inventor has, at some point in their life, suffered from what you are feeling right now. But never fear! The dreaded*

Inventor's Block has a simple cure: The Upside-Down Pose.'

I looked up at Broccoli, who shrugged. I continued reading.

'Research has shown that being upside down can improve blood flow to your brain, which can spark off an explosion of brand-new genius ideas.'

I slammed the book shut in excitement. 'Of course!' I cried. 'Why didn't I think of that?'

'ESHA!' came my sister's voice through the door. 'If I hear you shout one more time, I'm going to come in there and dismantle whatever it is you're inventing.'

I glared at the door.

One word about Nishi: **IGNORAMUS.**

Broccoli has interrupted to tell me that you need to know more about my sister, Nishi. He seems to think that 'she's a DRONG/ignoramus' isn't enough information, especially because of what happened with – well, you'll find out soon enough.

After thinking about it, I suppose that he is sort-of-maybe right, so I have made a list of the top six things you need to know about my big sister.

Feel free to skip it entirely.

You can still skip it.

Just miss the next page. It's that easy.

Top Six Things You Should Know About Nishi:

1. Nishi is exactly three years, two months, one day, six hours, 2.5 minutes and 0.4 seconds older than me. According to Nishi, this gives her full and total rights to boss me around.

2. To the rest of the world, she looks like this:

She ACTUALLY looks like this:

③ When Nishi is older, she wants to be a meteorologist. This is just a fancy way of saying she wants to bore people about the weather. She is boggly about the weather.

④ Nishi desperately wants to join the Guild of Junior Meteorologists (GUM for short). Unfortunately for her, she can't become a member until she passes the GUM exams, and she has already failed them twice.

⑤ She chews gum all the time. I am not quite sure if this has anything to do with passing the GUM exams. Nishi tells me that it does not, but I am not sure if I believe her.

(6) Nishi wears the same wellingtons everywhere. They are bright purple and covered with yellow umbrellas. They are also signed by Nimbus Dewey, the world's most famous meteorologist – Nishi's hero (yawn-boring-yawn). Nishi is so in love with these foulsome foot coverings that she wears them IN ALL WEATHERS. This means that they are less wellington and more **TOXIC WEAPON**.

'I bet Einstein didn't have to put up with a wit-nit of a sister,' I muttered. 'Bet he didn't have everyone interfering with his **grand ideas** every single minute of every single day.'

I passed Broccoli the *Inventor's Handbook*, positioned myself between Sock Mountains 3 and 4 and flipped myself on to my hands. [If you, the Reader, have never tried the Upside-Down Pose, it makes the world appear a little less **TOPSY** and a lot more **TURVEY**.]

'Any brain sparks?' asked Broccoli.

'Not yet. I think what I really need is a few moments without anyone—'

'**ESHA VERMA!**'

Ever so slowly, I opened one eye and saw Dad's slippers in the doorway. (Clearly, he did not have any respect for the sign that

said I was **NOT TO BE DISTURBED.**)

I opened my other eye and looked up at Dad's face. He did not appear surprised to see me upside down.

'What do you call this?' he said, holding a T-shirt out in front of him.

Dad's eyebrows waggled at me as he spoke. This was not good. Whenever Dad was cross, his eyebrows would start dancing uP and down. At that moment, they looked as if they were ready to take part in the

$$\text{Olympic}\ \ \overset{\text{H}}{\underset{\text{H}}{\overset{\text{G}}{\text{I}}}}\ \ \text{Ju}^\text{m}\text{p.}$$

I stared at the T-shirt. 'Y-E-L-M-U-B,' I said slowly. Dad snorted and turned the T-shirt upside down. What it should have said was the name of Dad's favourite football team: Burnley FC. Except there was a giant splodge zig-zagging across the letters.

'BUMLEY FC,' I said.

Dad flinched. 'I found this on top of it.' He waved a plastic bag containing a grape-coloured jelly goo at me. 'It was in the wash basket. Would you like to explain how it got there?'

Broccoli must have guessed that Dad was about to explode. Right on cue, he sneezed. Once. Twice. Three times.

No help there, then.

'Well, I—' I couldn't tell him that the grape-coloured jelly goo was the second prototype of the INSTA DE-STICKER SPRAY. It must have accidentally fallen out of my pocket when Mum put my special Inventioning dungarees in the wash basket. (I have warned her not to touch my stuff but she does not listen.) Quickly, I ran through the list of **Excuses for Parents** that I had memorized from the *Inventor's Handbook* when I was just five years old:

- EXCUSE 1: **Blame the dog** (No good – we don't have a dog because Mum is allergic. I didn't realize that until it was too late, but you live and learn).

- EXCUSE 2: **Blame next door's dog** (Also no good – Broccoli lived on one side and he had exactly **zero** dogs. On the other side was Claudette and her pet canary, Mister E, but he had been cage-bound for the last week because of a cold).

- EXCUSE 3: **Where no dogs are available, blame a brother/ sister/cousin/baby/grandparent.**

$$\boxed{\text{BINGO.}}$$

'You should talk to Nishi,' I said.

'Nishi?' said Dad, his eyebrows halting mid-waggle.

'I saw it in her room the other day.' I paused, pretending to think. 'She said it was for a weather experiment.'

The *Inventor's Handbook* calls this "**The Art of**

Persuasion: a must-have skill for any **genius inventor**. I call it an *ESHA NINJA BLOW*. For some reason, it appears to work on everyone but my DRONG of a sister.

'What kind of weather experiment?' said Dad, his eyebrows returning to full jiggle mode.

Before I could answer, Mum poked her head round the door.

(*Honestly, how is a genius inventor meant to get anything done when everyone keeps interfering?*)

'What is happening here?' asked Mum, waving her phone crossly. 'Aunty Usha is trying to give me her shopping list and — Esha why are you upside down? Oh, hello, Broccoli, I didn't see you there. I should have some lettuce for Archibald— what is *that*?' she finished, her eyes popping when she saw Dad's T-shirt.

Broccoli sneezed again.

I was about to move on to EXCUSE 4 when Mum stopped looking so cross and started laughing.

'Bumley FC,' she giggled. 'I couldn't have put it better myself.'

Dad's eyebrows disappeared into his hair.

'They're better than MAN-CHEESY UNITED,' he said.

Mum's face turned a dangerous shade of purple.

If you hadn't already guessed, my parents are **BOGGLY** ??? about football. Neither Nishi nor I understand it. It is probably the one thing in the world we agree on.

When Mum and Dad start arguing about football, it is usually a good time to make a quick exit. Unfortunately, that was not possible at that moment because:

① They were standing in my room.

② I was upside down.

I decided to wait. I don't know how long I ended up waiting in the end. Broccoli said it was only a couple of minutes, but I'm sure he lost track of time because I started to feel . . . *dizzy*. Maybe it was the smell of the carpet (sticky sweet jalebis with a hint of mango lassi) or keeping one eye on the door for Archibald (I was quite certain that he would try to make a run for it).

 jalebis

Either way, I'd had enough of the Upside-Down Pose for one day and I was about to flip myself the right way up when Mum said, 'I don't need a time machine to tell you how BUMLEY are going to do this year. They'll be **last** as always.'

It was as if I'd been jolted by an electric current.

A toe-tingling, hair-curling, brain-whizzying spark of

PURE GENIUS.

I was so excited that my arms turned to jelly, and I collapsed onto Sock Mountain 3, which let off a blast of toxic fumes.

'I've got it!' I shouted, pulling a spaghetti-encrusted sock out of my mouth. 'A TIME MACHINE! That's what will win us the Brain Trophy!'

When Mum had stopped choking from the sock smell, she said, 'Esha Verma, if you do not tidy this room today, you will be in BIG TROUBLE.'

When Dad stopped gagging, he said, 'Where's Nishi? I want to have a word with her about my T-shirt.'

And when Broccoli stopped sneezing he simply said, 'A time machine doesn't sound very safe.' Then, with an extra-enormous sniff, 'Where's Archibald?'

One scheming tortoise rescue later (he'd made it halfway down the stairs), I realized that the trouble with grand ideas is not just that they are one in a gazillion. The real trouble with grand ideas is that people just don't appreciate them.

Note From The Author (again)

Broccoli has just told me that I have spent **too long** getting to the start of this story. He thinks that I should have started with the chapter called **The Big Red Button**. I have told him that I wouldn't have taken as long if he stopped *interrupting* me.

As for you, Reader, you could skip to **The Big Red Button** right now but then you'll never find out how to invent a time machine.

And I'm SURE you want to know that,

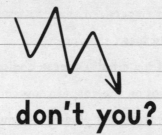

don't you?

How to Build a Time Machine – the Top-secret Method

OK, I lied. I'm not going to tell you how to build a time machine. Rule 3 of the *Inventor's Handbook* says that a **great inventor NEVER** reveals their secrets. What I can say is that it took us:

1. LOTS and **LOTS** of **TIME**
2. One hundred and ten visits to the library and the Science Museum
3. Fifty-three cycle rides to the rubbish dump
4. Three SECRET runs to Broccoli's garage
5. Twenty midnight raids on the kitchen
6. Ten careful rummages through Broccoli's stash of dangerous presents
7. Three burnt fingers
8. Two stubbed toes
9. Forty-five (and a half) cheese and chocolate sandwiches
10. Ten oil-stains on the carpet (now carefully hidden beneath strategically placed sock mountains)
11. One lightly toasted canary (how could we have known that Mister E from next door would fly into my room on the day we were fitting the fuel tank?)

The Big Red Button

At last, with only **ONE DAY** left before the contest, I, Esha Verma, **genius inventor extraordinaire**, was finally ready to test the **TIME MACHINE.** I'd waited until Mum and Dad had left to do Aunty Usha's shopping. Technically, I wasn't supposed to test any inventions when they weren't at home. *Practically*, I knew that it was better to trial inventions without their knowledge. That way Broccoli could clear up any mess if things didn't *quite* go according to plan. Inventioning is an unpredictable business, after all.

I am sure you are **FOOT-HOPPINGLY** desperate to know what ~~my~~ our time machine looked like, so I have included a picture below:

If you were reading carefully, you will remember that Rule 3 of the *Inventor's Handbook* says that: A great inventor **NEVER** reveals their secrets. So you'll just have to use your imagination.

TOP SECRET ★

There were only FOUR things left to do before the contest TOMORROW:

1. Plug in the power cable.
2. Cross fingers.
3. Cross toes.
4. Cross everything else.

Broccoli uncoiled the GIANT power cable and handed it to me with a nervous glance.

I plugged the wall-end into the power socket and took the other end over to the time machine.

'This is it,' I said to Broccoli, my fingers and toes tingling with excitement. 'If this works, we'll absolutely win the **Brain Trophy** tomorrow.'

'What if it doesn't?' asked Broccoli.

I snorted. 'Course it will. We've double-checked the wiring, triple-checked the connections and quadruple-checked our calculations.' I took a deep breath and grinned. 'Do you smell that, Broccoli? That's the odour of VICTORY.'

Broccoli sniffed and wrinkled his nose. 'Smells like **SOCKS**.'

I pretended not to hear him. 'This time tomorrow, I'll win the Brain Trophy and NOTHING is going to stop me. Now, are you ready?'

'I don't know.' He sniffed. His eyes were two round puddles and his nose was dripping like a tap. He was a walking, talking waterworks. 'What if it sends us back in time? Or forward? Or sideways?'

'We're only powering it up,' I said, waving the cable in the air. 'It won't do anything until we press The Big Red Button.'

Archibald yawned, trying his hardest not to look curious.

I touched my Inventor's Thinking Hat for luck.

It was the moment that all great inventors wait for. That spingly second when you're standing on the very edge of a grand discovery of great importance. This was the moment that could turn me into an inventor legend for eternity. I could see it all: the roaring crowds, mountains of money, my very own inventor's workshop . . .

Broccoli sniffed loudly behind me.

~~Maybe even a new apprenti—~~ ha ha ha

I plugged the power cable into the time machine and crossed everything.

And waited.

And waited.

And **waited** some more.

'Are you sure this was the biggest power cable—' I started to say to Broccoli when there was an

ENORMOUS WHUMP.

The **WHUMP** was more than a noise. It was a tidal wave of sonic power. It bubbled the blood in my veins, rattled my teeth and sent Broccoli's snot cascading through the air onto the walls where it slid down with a loud glop.

He sniffed and wiped his nose apologetically.

I shuddered. 'EW . . .'

Before Broccoli could reply, Nishi stormed into my room, a toxic wellington whiff wafting around her.

'That's IT,' she shouted. 'My first GUM exam is TOMORROW and I can't even THINK about compass navigation when all I can hear is—'

But I wasn't listening to her.

I was looking at the time machine, which was

whirring and humming

behind her.

I gawped at the spinny dials on the console,

the swirling-whirling arrows

and the twirling-twisting

TIME-O-METER.

My heart did a little jump.

Out of the corner of my eye, I saw Broccoli shrink himself between Sock Mountains 3 and 4.

'I think it's ready,' I whispered.

This was it. My moment of greatn—

'—and Mum and Dad said you weren't allowed to test any inventions when they're not at home,' huffed Nishi. 'Especially after your last disaster.'

URGH. Moment ruined.

I glared at her. 'How was I supposed to know that the Self-Popping Party Poppers would explode through the kitchen roof?! Besides, the Young Inventor of the Year contest is *also* TOMORROW and I need to begin Trialling and Testing so will you get those toxic weapons—' I pointed at her wellingtons— 'and yourself out of my room? Your DRONGNESS is disturbing my genius vibes.'

Nishi wrinkled her nose at the time machine as if she could make it disappear with the power of her nostrils. 'What is this junk heap, anyway?' she said. 'A hoover?'

What did I tell you about my sister? No imagination.

'*That* is OBVIOUSLY a time machine,' I said.

Nishi let out a noise that sounded like a wheezy cat. 'There's NO such thing.'

I raised my eyebrows and gave her my best DOES-IT-LOOK-LIKE-I'M-JOKING stare.

Nishi folded her arms and gave me her best I-know-better-than-you stare. 'I thought you wanted to win the Brain Trophy, not the Worst Disaster of the Year Award.'

'Oh, I think you'll win *that* one,' I said lightly, 'when you fail the GUM exams AGAIN.'

I heard Broccoli take a sharp breath behind me.

Archibald made an excited sniggering noise, which sounded like tortoise-speak for, 'here we go'.

Nishi's mouth flapped open-closed-open and her eyeballs bulged like an animal about to stampede. I braced myself and prepared to take cover behind Sock Mountain 3.

But she didn't move towards me.

Instead, she leapt the other way.

TOWARDS the time machine.

Before I could stop her, she'd jumped on to the seat (a *borrowed* bike saddle) and started

pressing her fingers
ALL
OVER
THE CONSOLE.

'STOP!' I yelled. 'You don't know what you're doing!' I dived forward, every one of my **genius** instincts screaming to push her off, then stopped suddenly – what if we damaged the time machine?

'You don't know what YOU'RE doing,' retorted Nishi. She jabbed another button. 'Just because you've got an *Inventor's Handbook*, it doesn't make you an inventor. Anyone with even a smidge of a brain knows that time travel is impossible.'

'Not as impossible as you trying to navigate anything with a compass or predict the weather,' I snapped, wondering how I could **wrestle** her off the time machine without breaking the console.

Broccoli whimpered.

Nishi scowled and twisted a spinny dial. 'At least meteorology is a *real* science!'

'Inventioning is more of a science than silly cloud watching!' I said, glancing around my room for the **Extend-a-Hand**. Wrestling Nishi off the time machine was too risky but maybe I could **BOP** her off it instead. 'Inventioning is—'

'A WASTE OF TIME,' interrupted Nishi.

'GENIUS. Isn't that right, Broccoli?' I said, signalling him to find the **Extend-a-Hand**.

Broccoli blinked at me, confused, and held up a sock.

Honestly.

'GENIUS?' Nishi snorted. She took a packet of gum  out of her pocket and flicked one into her mouth. 'This thing is **useless.** I bet you my GUM binoculars –' she waved them in my face as she spoke – 'that your so-called invention won't work.' She pressed another button. The time machine gurgled like a happy baby.

I clenched my fists. 'You're **USELESS!**'

I knew at once I'd made a mistake.

'Oh, **AM I?**' said Nishi.

That's when she did something really very stupid.

She put her hand over the centre of the console.

'Don't **YOU DARE,**' I said sharply.

Nishi gave me an **EVIL** grin.

Then she pressed

THE
BIG RED
BUTTON.

A note from Broccoli

Dear Reader, if you prefer safe and sensible stories, now would be a good moment to put this book down and forget everything you have read so far. If, like me, you are training to become a genius inventor, then you should continue.

Be warned: the happenings you will read about in the coming pages are not for the faint-hearted. Unfortunately, I had no choice but to face them armed with nothing but my wits and my loyal tortoise companion, Archibald.

Secondus Secondi

For a moment, nothing happened.

'Ha!' exclaimed Nishi. 'What did I tell—'

Before she could finish speaking, the time machine made a funny gurgling noise like the plug being pulled out of a bath. The power cable **exploded** out of the socket and snapped through the air like a shimmying snake, narrowly missing Broccoli, who dived into the sock mountain beside him.

Then **POP...** Nishi and the time machine were gone.

Only it was not a small POP. It was a very **LOUD POP**.

It was so *loud* that it flung open the windows, shook the floor beneath our feet and set off the car alarms outside. Sock Mountain 5 *trembled* then disappeared through a hole.

A very **LARGE** hole.

A very **LARGE** hole IN MY BEDROOM FLOOR.

UH-OH.

As inventions went, this should have rated as **NUMBER ONE** on my list of Accidental Disasters. But I was too excited to worry about that. Besides, I knew Mum and Dad wouldn't be back for hours yet, so we were safe for now.

'Did you *see* that?' I whispered to Broccoli. I looked at where Nishi had been. The air was still fizzing and sparking. One moment she'd been sitting on the bike saddle, the next she was **GONE**.

'I think . . . I think it worked!' I shouted, but then I paused, realizing something not *quite* so exciting.

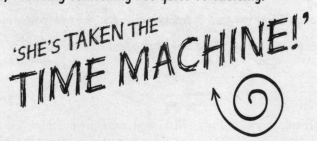
'SHE'S TAKEN THE TIME MACHINE!'

'But,' squeaked Broccoli. 'But-but-but—'
Before he could say anything else, the air in front of us started to do something very strange. It began to move. It rippled and **shook** like the air on a platform as a train comes in. Broccoli whimpered. I looked around my room for something to arm myself with when, suddenly, the *whooshing* stopped.

A moment later, a strange oval-shaped thing appeared in front of me.

SMELLS LIKE STRAWBERRIES

SHIMMERY STREAKS
OF BLUE AND
SILVER

SHINY PEA
GREEN
AIR AROUND IT
HUMMING

BUMPY LIKE TREE
BARK

Now, you, the Reader, may be wondering why I didn't just run out of there. But running away never entered my mind, not even for a second. At that moment, I was filled with **UNKNOWING.** My inventor's instincts were **tingling** to **TINGLEDOM** and all I could think about was the **ultra-genius** calculations that someone must have made to invent a thing that could appear in the air like this.

Besides, Chapter 8 of the *Inventor's Handbook* said that

inventors must always be ready for shocks and surprises, so I did not panic or leap down the stairs. To my surprise, Broccoli did not panic or run out of the room, either. But that might have been because he was frozen to the spot in **FEAR.**

[A note from Broccoli: I did, in fact, faint, for a minute or two.]

As I looked on, spellbound, a handle in the oval-shaped thing rattled, a door flew open and a boy stepped out.

BOWLER HAT

GOLD EYE RING
(BROCCOLI HAS JUST
TOLD ME THAT THE
PROPER NAME FOR
THIS IS MONOCLE)

RED TIE

WHITE SHIRT

SHINY RED
WAISTCOAT

STRIPY RED-AND-
WHITE BLAZER

PENCIL

RED TROUSERS

POLISHED
RED
SHOES

He lifted his bowler hat, brought out a tiny clipboard and raised his pencil to the page.

'Mission One,' he said, a smile of satisfaction spreading across his face. His pencil scratched across the paper. He licked the tip of his finger and held it in the air. 'The twenty-first century. Local time: fifteen-thirty hours.'

I looked at Broccoli. At least, I tried to look at Broccoli. He was still hidden behind a sock mountain. Archibald was watching the boy with a 'finally someone interesting' expression on his face.

'Local inhabitants,' said the boy. He looked at me, Archibald, then finally the cowering Broccoli. 'Two Minor Insignificants, one domesticated reptile.' He spoke lightning-bolt fast as if he had too much to do and not enough time to get it done. 'Let's see now.' He pulled out a shiny red book labelled

'TOOT TOOT: TALK FOR TOOTERS' and squinted at the first page. Suddenly he swivelled on the spot and lifted one leg in the air. 'Wazooki!' he shouted.

I blinked.

'No?' He turned the page. 'Ah.' Holding his hand in the air, he looked at me and wiggled his fingers. 'Howdy, partner!'

I stared at him.

'Hm.' He frowned and turned a few more pages. He scrunched his mouth into a peculiar shape, closed one eye and staggered sideways. 'Ahoy, landlubbers. Shiver me timbers. ARRRRR.'

I couldn't help it. I giggled. 'What?'

'Salutations and greetings,' said the boy. He scratched his head. 'Funny, the Academy told us they'd work.' He made a note on his clipboard. 'I'll have to speak to T.O.O.T. Talk Tech.'

'TOOT?' I sniggered.

The boy puffed himself up like a balloon and straightened his hat. 'The Office of Time is no joke,' he said sharply.

'I am Secondus Secondi, a New Officer of Time.'

'Who?'

'Secondus Secondi,' said the boy again proudly. 'Son of Dayus Secondi and Yearma Secondi, grandson of Epochal Secondi, great-grandson of Centurio Secondi, and so forth.'

I noticed he'd forgotten to ask me who I was. Good thing I'd memorized Chapter 1 of the *Inventor's Handbook*: Introducing Your Genius Self.

'My name is Esha Verma, **genius inventor extraordinaire**, youngest and best daughter of Anita and Rohan Verma, granddaughter of Dharam Verma, great-granddaughter of . . .' I faltered.

Actually, I couldn't quite remember that far back. It's very difficult to keep track of family trees as big as mine when your mind is full of **genius**.

'. . . Of another Very Important Verma and *this* –' I pointed to the quivering pile of socks behind me – 'is my apprentice, Broccoli. He's in training.'

A hand appeared in the air and waved shakily. 'Pleased to meet you,' squeaked a muffled voice.

Secondus raised an eyebrow and made a note. 'I'm here because we detected an **unusual** spike in **TIME ENERGY**,' he said.

'As an Officer of Time, it is my job to investigate and resolve such matters.' He turned round and eyed the space where the time machine had been. All that was left of ~~my~~ our invention was honey-coloured goop on the carpet.

Broccoli poked his head out from behind the socks to watch. Secondus bent down beside the goop and sniffed it.

'What are you doing?' I asked.

goop

'Silence, please,' said Secondus as he wrote on his clipboard. 'I am in the middle of an **important** inspection.'

'What kind of inspection?'

Secondus tutted and ignored me. He took out a thin brass device. As he held it in the spot where the time machine had been, the device started to emit a loud ticking noise. 'How peculiar,' said Secondus. He made *another* note on his clipboard.

'Because if this is about our time machine then—'

'Time machine?' interrupted

Secondus. He stood up so quickly that his hat wobbled like a runaway strawberry.

'What time machine?'

'The time machine I— I mean, we **invented**,' I said proudly. 'Except now it's gone.'

'That *can't* be right . . .' said Secondus. He flicked through the paper on his clipboard, muttering to himself. 'Time machine . . . time machine . . . time— ah.' He squinted at the clipboard then he checked the brass device, which was still ticking. 'Mighty clocks! Energy readings are an exact match. But time machines aren't supposed to have been invented yet. It's too **EARLY!**'

'Weren't you listening?' I flicked an invisible speck of dust off my sleeve. 'I am a **genius inventor extraordinaire.** We are always ahead of our time. Isn't that right, Broccoli?'

The sock mountain nodded.

'You must have a permit to build a time machine,' said Secondus.

I blinked. 'What permit?'

He cleared his throat. 'Section 4.2, Regulation 2.6 of Time-travel Devices: any time-travel devices can only be invented or used *after* getting a permit from The Office of Time. Failure to have a permit will result in T.O.O.T.-decreed punishment, which may include a **fine**, imprisonment or any other suitable sentence.'

He nodded at Broccoli, who promptly sneezed. 'These regulations also apply to apprentices.'

Archibald snickered.

'**A FINE?**' I shouted. (That was about the only thing of his entire YAWN-BORING-YAWN speech that I had understood.) Dad was still recovering from the Self-Popping Party Poppers disaster. What would he say when I told him he had to pay out for a time machine that Nishi had stolen? 'But I didn't know about any regulations. Besides, we can't go to The Office of Time. I want to find my sister.'

OK, so maybe I lied. I didn't really *want* to find my sister. I could think of many reasons why Nishi being lost in time wasn't a bad thing. What I REALLY wanted was my our machine back. There was absolutely not enough time to build another one for tomorrow's contest. And there was not a pipsqueakity chance that I was going to lose the Brain Trophy just because my DRONG of a sister couldn't do as she was told.

'I'm afraid the Time Regulations overrule lost siblings, spectacles, socks, pets, pencils, keys, kites, etcetera, etcetera,' said Secondus.

'But she's LOST IN TIME,' I said. 'Doesn't The Office of Time have regulations about that?'

Secondus blinked. 'Lost in Time?'

'That's what I said.'

Secondus's mouth opened and closed like a fish. 'You said your time machine was gone,' he squeaked.

'Because my IGNORAMUS of a sister, Nishi,

STOLE IT.'

The Lost-in-time Protocol
(and a lesson in The Art of Persuasion)

'A "Lost in Time" is a Class Three emergency,' said
Secondus hoarsely. He flipped furiously through the papers
on his clipboard, muttering to himself. 'Extremely rare,
extremely dangerous—'

'DANGEROUS?' whimpered Broccoli.

'Here it is!' said Secondus. 'The Lost-in-time
Protocol.' His eyes darted across the clipboard.
'Step one – speak to local inhabitants to locate the
whenabouts of the "Lost in Time".' He looked at me
expectantly. 'Do you know when your sister has gone?'

'How would I know that?'

'Did you fit the machine with a time lock? A back-
trace? Anything we could use to find her? You built this
machine – didn't you consider this?'

I scowled. It was one thing for my DRONG of a sister
to steal my our time machine and my our best chance of
winning the Brain Trophy. Now this boy was talking to
me as if I was an ignoramus.

'It's the first one we've ever built,' I said. 'I hadn't even put it through Trialling and Testing yet!'

'Mighty grand clocks!' exclaimed Secondus, his hat dancing in outrage.

He dabbed his forehead with a handkerchief and looked down at the clipboard. His lips moved in silent concentration. After a moment, he slipped the clipboard under his hat and stepped over the goop. Holding his monocle to his eye, he moved his head up, down and sideways, as if he were looking for something. 'They'd better be here,' he whispered, his nose crinkled in worry.

'What are you doing?' asked Broccoli, eyeing the goop.

'Quiet,' whispered Secondus. Very slowly, he pulled a tiny glass vial out of his waistcoat. Standing on his tiptoes, he uncorked the stopper and then, in one grand swoop, he swept the vial across the air and hurriedly stuck the stopper back into the vial.

'Got them!' he cried triumphantly.

I breathed in sharply.

The empty vial was now filled with lots of wriggling blobs.

'What are those?' squeaked Broccoli.

'They look like glow-worms,' I said, staring at them in wonder.

'Glow-worms?' exclaimed Secondus. 'Don't be ridiculous. These are tocks.' They were tiny, less than half a thumb-length in size. Each tock was a bedazzling, glittering pink and had thin silvery-grey wings. They flew inside the vial, making an angry *trizz trizz* noise as they hit the glass.

'Tocks?' said Broccoli. For someone who was **BOGGLY** about bloodthirsty reptiles, I noticed he was leaning as far away from these tiny tocks as he possibly could. He was so far back he looked as if he were in the middle of a backwards somersault. 'Are they **DANGEROUS?'**

'Dangerous?' Secondus scoffed. 'Tocks? Mighty clocks! You really don't know much, do you?' He closed one eye and pressed the other to the glass, squinting in fierce concentration. 'When something travels through time, it creates a rush of **time energy**,' he said haughtily. 'It's invisible, of course, but tocks smell it from light years away. They'll race to feed on it before it disappears and then they'll be gone. You have to be quick to catch them.'

At the bottom of the glass was a small pile of dust. As I looked closer, I realized the dust was coming out of the tocks in thin, shimmering curls.

'What is that?' I asked, fascinated.

'Time trails,' said Secondus, his eye stuck to the glass like a limpet. 'Whatever Tocks can't digest they— there it is!' he exclaimed suddenly, his hat dancing so ferociously I was certain it was about to take off. The dust at the bottom of the glass had started to gleam a brilliant silvery-blue. He whipped out a ruler and held it against the vial. 'Grand clocks!' His eyes widened. 'Your sister's travelled to the Cretaceous Age.'

Broccoli made a strange squealing noise and leapt out of the sock mountain. My **Extend-a-Hand** flew into the air and landed by my feet. *So that's where it was.* 'Did you say Cretaceous?' he said.

??? ??? ??? ???

'**Cretaceous?**' I stared at him in surprise, wondering how exactly he knew something I didn't. 'What's the—?' I started.

'The Cretaceous Age,' said Broccoli. 'The last and longest period of the Mesozoic Era, the Age of the Reptiles!'

'The Age of the . . . but that means—'

'Dinosaurs,' said Broccoli, his snot

bouncing around faster than a jelly in an earthquake. He held

Archibald in front of his face
so that he was looking him
in the eye. 'Can you believe
it, Archie? Dinosaurs! Imagine
what Granny Bertha would say!'

Archibald made a noise that could have been 'why the human and *not me*'.

I could not believe my ears.

I, Esha Verma, **genius inventor extraordinaire**, had invented a time machine that could send someone to the Age of the Reptiles. Of course, I had never had any doubt. **Not really.**

I could already see myself winning the Brain Trophy. Hear Mum and Dad boasting about their favourite daughter. Smell my beautiful new multimillion-pound laboratory where my DRONG of a sister could not—

My daydream **burst** like a **balloon**.

In my excitement, I'd forgotten that Nishi had **TAKEN the time machine.**

'Did you know there are millions and millions of years in the Cretaceous Age?' continued Broccoli. '*Dinosaur World* says—'

'That's exactly why I must get this over to the Chief Finder immediately,' interrupted Secondus, scribbling on the clipboard. He shoved the vial into his pocket and straightened his hat. 'Time trails are only approximations. Once I have the exact time-landing coordinates, I'll be able to find your sister . . . as long as she hasn't been . . .

EATEN.'

I scoffed. 'No dinosaur would want to eat Nishi. Not in those wellingtons. They'd only get food poisoning.' At least I HOPED they wouldn't. The last thing I needed was for Mum and Dad to **ban** me from INVENTIONING just because my DRONG of a sister had got herself digested.

'Could she use the time machine to bring herself back?' asked Secondus.

I thought for a second. 'Not unless she can find a power socket. I was planning to take batteries with us, but—'

'Has she been **stabilized?**' he interrupted.

'Stabilized?' I echoed.

'So that's a no,' said Secondus, his pencil thumping the clipboard.

'What exactly do you—'

'How long has she been gone?'

I shrugged in exasperation. 'About five minutes.'

'Five minutes!' echoed Secondus shrilly. He scribbled hastily across the clipboard, his eyes steely with determination. 'There's not a moment to lose. If your sister hasn't been **chomped** or **crushed**, the Butterfly Ripples could already be taking effect.'

'Butterfly Ripples?' echoed Broccoli, staring at me in horror. 'They're real?'

'We've read about those,' I said to Secondus smugly.

'Grand clocks, of course they're real,' snapped Secondus, already hurrying towards his egg-shaped machine. His hat bounced like a jittery bug. 'Certain actions in one time zone could affect another in ways you can't even imagine! That's why we're ALWAYS stabilized before travel.'

'But-but-but we didn't prepare for—' gabbled Broccoli.

'I must find and stabilize her, deactivate the time machine and—'

⟶ 'DEACTIVATE IT?' I said sharply.

Archibald guffawed, his shell trembling with laughter.

'Section 2, Regulation 4.5 of Time-travel Devices: all

illegal time-travel devices must be deactivated before being impounded. You'll be held here in a Frozen Moment until I return.'

I g°ggled at him. No way was I going to let this bowler-hat-wearing boy DEACTIVATE or IMPOUND ~~my~~ our time machine.

'You CAN'T deactivate it,' I said.

'Section 2, Regulation 1.1 of Time Policies and Principles: officers have the power to—'

'No, I mean you CAN'T,' I said, my brain SPARKING with a HOW-TO-SOLVE-THIS-PROBLEM IDEA. 'The deactivation console is fingerprint controlled.'

'Fingerprint controlled?' said Secondus, halting in his tracks.

'I don't remember—' started Broccoli.

'Only we can deactivate it,' I said, giving Broccoli a "now is not the time" look.

Secondus scrunched up his eyebrows, his forehead crumpling in worry. 'If I transport it without deactivating it first, its time energy could blow my navigation systems . . .'

I shrugged, preparing my ESHA NINJA BLOW. 'Don't say I didn't warn you when everything goes

KAPOOSH.'

Secondus was silent for a moment.

'And only the two of you can deactivate it?' he said.

BINGO.

'It's an Inventor–Apprentice double thumb lock. You can read about it in Chapter 18 of the *Inventor's Handbook* if you like.'

Archibald widened his eyes in a look that probably meant 'impressive sneakiness for a human'.

'**Mighty grand clocks**,' said Secondus. 'The Academy never told us about those.' He dabbed his forehead again and took a deep breath. 'Very well. Section 2, Regulation 3.5 of Time Policies and Principles allows passengers to accompany officers for mission-critical reasons. You will have to come with me.'

'We will?' I said, hiding my grin.

'**WE WILL?**' squeaked Broccoli in panic.

'We find and stabilize your sister, deactivate and impound the machine, then I take you to Headquarters.'

Of course, I was *obviously* going to save ~~my~~ our time machine, but I nodded. Chapter 58 of the *Inventor's Handbook* said that solving a complicated problem was like peeling an onion. One layer at a time.

'You have one Earth minute to organize any urgent affairs before we leave,' said Secondus, hotfooting towards his machine. 'These time trails won't give off a smell forever.'

'I don't think we should do this,' whimpered Broccoli. 'Maybe he should find Nishi himself.'

'And what about the **time machine?**' I said, pulling him away so that Secondus couldn't hear what we were saying. 'The Young Inventor of the Year contest is **TOMORROW**. We have to find a way to bring it back before then. This is **our chance to win** the Brain Trophy.'

Broccoli's nose trembled. 'What about deactivating it?'

I snorted. 'We're not deactivating it.'

'But how—'

'I don't know yet,' I said, 'but I'll figure it out.'

Broccoli bit his lip. 'It doesn't sound very safe.'

I prodded him in the chest. 'You, James Bertha Darwin, are the grandson of the bravest fossil hunter in the world. Do you think she would **refuse** a chance to

TRAVEL THROUGH TIME?'

Broccoli shook his head. 'No, but—'

'Do you think she would **refuse** a chance to travel to the AGE OF THE DINOSAURS?'

'**Never,**' said Broccoli, his nose twitching.

'Don't you, James Bertha Darwin, want to see them too?'

Broccoli hesitated, long enough for me to grab his copy of *Dinosaur World* out of his pocket. 'Look,' I said, waving it at him, 'this is your chance to see them for real.'

Broccoli took hold of the magazine and stared at the front cover. 'You're right,' he said. 'And I suppose, if we're careful and sensible—'

Archibald made a rude noise at the back of his throat.

'In any case,' I said, priming my second *ESHA NINJA BLOW*. 'You signed an agreement. Don't you remember the small print? It says that you, James Bertha Darwin, **must** accompany me in all expeditions or adventures required BEFORE, DURING OR AFTER INVENTIONING.'

Actually, I couldn't quite remember if the agreement did say this or if there even was any small print. In fact, at that moment, I couldn't even remember where I'd put the agreement, but luckily Broccoli didn't ask for it. Instead, he took a deep breath and said, 'If we're travelling back in time, we're going to need **supplies**.'

I grinned. 'You're right.'

I picked up my **Extend-a-Hand**, then, looking around the room, I grabbed my *Inventor's Handbook* and jammed my Inventor's Thinking Hat on to my head. Finally, I double-checked my pocket to make sure my Inventor's Kit was inside. 'Ready.'

'That's your Earth minute,' said Secondus, poking his head out of the machine.

Broccoli sneezed, slid his copy of *Dinosaur World* into his pocket, checked that the Screeching Fizzer Firecracker was still in his other pocket, sneezed again then looked at Archibald. 'Are you ready, Archie?'

'We're not taking *him*,' I said.

'Tortoises belong to the same reptile family as dinosaurs,' said Broccoli. 'This is his chance to meet his ancestors. I can't leave him behind.'

Archibald gave me his most **cunning** smile.

I snorted. 'You'll have to keep an eye on him,' I said, hurrying after Secondus. 'I'm not TORTOISE-SITTING when I have a time machine to find.'

'We'll be fine, won't we, Archie?' said Broccoli, stumbling after me. 'Totally fine. What could possibly **go**

w r o n g?'

A Disclaimer to the Reader of this Journal

(included on the instructions of Secondus Secondi, New Officer of Time, representative of T.O.O.T.)

This disclaimer hereby forewarns the Reader. By continuing to read this journal, the Reader accepts that neither I, Secondus Secondi, New Officer of Time, nor T.O.O.T., will be held responsible for any and all reactions of amazement, wonder or mind-befuddlement that may arise as a result of reading the information in this journal.

Complaints dealing with such matters will be returned unopened.

We thank you for your cooperation now, then and in the future.

Signed:

Secondus Secondi

Through the Door

I am absolutely sure that, like me, you, the Reader, must also be foot-hoppingly desperate to find out what was behind the door of the machine Secondus arrived in. Unfortunately, Broccoli had forgotten to pack a camera, so you will have to use this drawing to **imagine**

the **gob-dropping**

eye-popping

gut-curling

hair-whirling

WONDERMAZEMENT of what we saw.

The Perombulator

'Shut the door and **don't touch** anything,' said
Secondus, leaping between buttons and switches.

'What *is* this thing?' whimpered Broccoli behind me.

'My Perombulator,' said Secondus proudly.

I g°ggled as I looked around. 'But it's
ENORMOUS. How did you get it inside my room?'

'An Officer of Time is specially trained for **difficult
landings**,' boasted Secondus. He jabbed a device marked
RIPPLE METER. At the bottom was a silver butterfly-shaped
dial. Suddenly the dial flashed pink, humming softly. 'Thank
the clocks.' His scowl lifted a little. 'No ripples detected across
the Cretaceous Age yet.' He stopped suddenly as he
caught sight of Archibald. 'Is the reptile coming too?'

'We can't leave him,' said Broccoli, holding tightly on to
Archibald. 'He's my responsibility.'

Archibald made a low snicking noise, which was probably
tortoise-speak for 'the human knows nothing'.

'Just keep him away from the Primary Console,' said Secondus

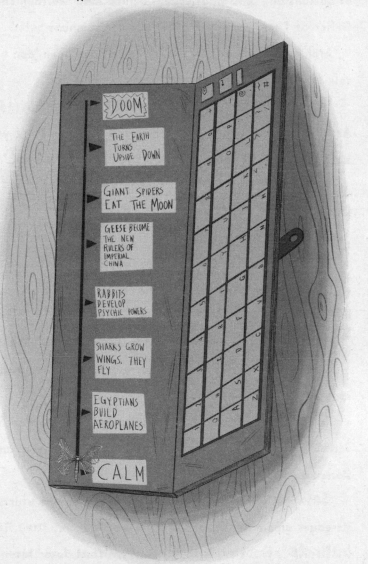

with a dismissive sigh, waving a hand at the bonkers arrangement of buttons and dials and screens behind him. 'Neither The Office of Time, nor I, will offer any replacement pets.'

Archibald made a noise, which could have been 'don't talk to me about human pets. I never wanted one'.

'**Replacement pets?**' gulped Broccoli. He lifted Archibald to his face and looked him in the eye. 'Don't you worry, Archie,' he said. 'I won't let you out of my sight.'

Archibald flicked his front feet in what I absolutely know to be a *RUDE gesture*.

[A note from Broccoli: It is not.]

'If we're travelling through time, wouldn't it be easier to go back and stop Nishi pressing the red button on the time machine?' I pointed out.

'And create a time paradox?' said Secondus with a LOUD snort.

Clearly, The Office of Time had not taught him how to speak to **genius inventors**.

He pushed a sequence of different buttons. A motor labelled SENSORS began to *spin* above his head. He darted past us and slotted a device into the centre of the steering wheel.

'**Sat-Nav,**' I read over his shoulder. The device whirred, its edges gleaming. I reached out towards it, my **inventor's instincts** trembling with curiosity. 'What does this—'

'**Grand clocks!**' shouted Secondus, batting my hand away. 'This is a **Space and Time Navigation** device.' He jabbed a finger at a brass plaque fixed to the top of the device:

> **WARNING:**
> **ONLY TO BE USED**
> **BY AN OFFICER**
> **OF TIME.**

I gave him my best *ESHA LASER GLARE.*

Unfortunately, Secondus was too distracted turning arrows on the Sat-Nav (else he would have started sweating buckets). Before I could try again, a loud hum ran through the Perombulator's walls.

'What's happening?' whimpered Broccoli. His face had turned a peculiar porridge-like colour. I wondered if I should have brought a stinky sock to wave over his nose in case he fainted.

A moment later, the Perombulator began to shake.

'I hope your sister arrived in one piece,' murmured Secondus, frowning at his clipboard. 'Put-backing can be a sticky business.'

Broccoli took a backwards step towards the door.

The sign pinged from **STANDBY** to **ACTIVE**. The humming grew louder. My **genius** instincts itched with excitement.

Broccoli whimpered and grabbed hold of my arm.

'There's no need to panic,' said Secondus.
'It's just the Perombulance.'

'Shouldn't you be steering?' gabbled
Broccoli.

'The Perombulator is auto-piloted,' said
Secondus. 'Manual control is only needed when—'

'I can't do this!' wailed Broccoli. 'I'm not like
Grandma. I don't have a single brave bone in my
body.'

Archibald rolled his eyes. For once, I agreed with him.

'Maybe you *should* stay—' I began to say only I didn't finish
because at that moment the air **EXPLODED**. It was like
the EAR-POPPING feeling you get when you're on a plane, only
this was a GAZILLION times worse.

My teeth TREMBLED.
My fingers FUMBLED.
My skull **SCROMBLED**.

The Perombulator shook as if there were a
THOUSAND RHINOS STAMPEDING over it. The
ship's wheel spun left-ways and right-ways. An opera-level

SHRIEK filled my eardrums as a Broccoli-shaped thing torpedoed past me. Out of the corner of my eye, I saw a thrilled tortoise-sized blob slide past in the opposite direction.

The air pressed down on us and I was sure I was going to be turned into a human pancake just because my DRONG of a sister couldn't listen to instructions when—

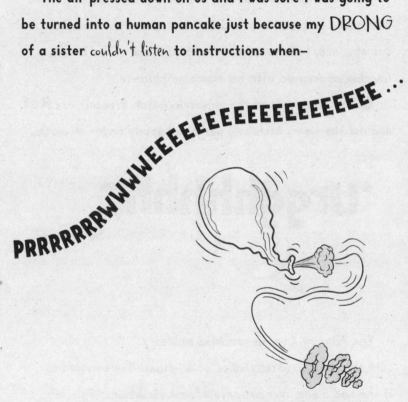

PRRRRRRRWWWEEEEEEEEEEEEEEEE...

There was a noise like the air escaping from a balloon. The Perombulator stopped shaking. My eyelids flipped back the right way and my stomach lifted itself out from between my toes.

Secondus was peering at a screen labelled PEROMBLE-O-METER. 'Speed – quadrillion quatrillion perombles—'

He didn't look as if he'd just escaped from being turned into a human pancake. He didn't even have a *single* hair out of place. I glowered at him, trying not to be a teensy-tiny bit impressed with his supreme balance.

On the other side of the Perombulator, Broccoli was **flat** against the floor, Archibald perched happily on his stomach.

'Urgghhhhh,'

he groaned.

The Primary Console crackled suddenly. 'TOOT TOOT,' said the clipped, nasally voice of a woman. She sounded as if she had a peg over her nose. 'Zonal conditions: Fair. No turbulence expected. We wish you safe travels. TOOT TOOT.'

I wobbled to the window, my heart thudding with curiosity.

Through the glass, I could see a

 gazillion sparks of light.

I watched as one of them floated closer.

It was a shifting rainbow of colour.

A kaleidoscopic ball of brilliance.

 A soaring shiny dot of luminosity.

'Broccoli, you have to come and see these lights,'
I murmured in awe. 'They're beautiful.'

'Those aren't lights,' said Secondus without turning
round. 'They're time-space particles. They're what the
Murkle is made from.'

'The Murkle?'

'All of time and space,' he said in exasperation.
'Do all Minor Insignificants ask so many questions?'

'Of course not,' I said, offended. 'Only genius inventors
such as myself. In fact, I'm specially trained to—'

'Uggghh,' moaned Broccoli again, a large sprout of snot dangling out of his nose. Archibald tucked his head back into his shell.

Secondus punched some buttons on the Primary Console. A jar to the left of his head began to rattle, a storm of colourful mist collecting inside it. I watched, SPELLBOUND, as the mist formed a ball. It dropped into a pipe and popped out of the other end into a slot labelled STABILIZERS. Using a pair of tiny tongs, Secondus held it out to Broccoli. 'Stabilizing sherbet,' he said. 'Effective for one Earth day. You are required to eat it.'

Broccoli stared at the sherbet with a worried look on his face.

It was entirely transparent, like the clearest window glass. On one side, in tiny letters, were etched the words: FOR RIPPLE-FREE TRAVEL.

'Ripple-free travel.' I echoed. 'What's inside it?'

Secondus turned his nose up at me.

'That's top secret.'

'Of course,' I said, smiling innocently. If he wouldn't tell me, I'd just wait for the right moment to find out for myself. After all, Chapter 17 of the *Inventor's Handbook* says that all great inventors must be ready to build their **genius** knowledge AT ALL TIMES.

Broccoli turned the sherbet over. The other side was marked

WARNING:

EXCLUSIONS APPLY.

'What exclusions?' he asked as Secondus turned back to the Primary Console.

'The permanent life-and-death kind,' he said with *utmost solemnity*. The jar rattled *fiercely* and another sherbet popped out of the slot. 'If you're *squashed* by a dinosaur, you'll cease to exist. If you're *fried* by a tunnel dragon, you'll cease to exist. If you're *caught in a Time Coil*, you'll—'

'**– Cease to exist,**' I snapped impatiently.

'– Cease to exist,' *whimpered* Broccoli.

At the centre of the sherbet was a perfectly round, wrinkly pip. The pip was a brilliant sun-orange, but it slowly swirled into a dangerous plum colour.

'It . . . it . . . *changed*,' *squeaked* Broccoli, holding the sherbet at arm's length. Archibald poked his head out of his shell to give Broccoli a "you are an embarrassing human" look.

Secondus looked at Broccoli as if he were the biggest **IGNORAMUS** he had ever met. 'Of course it changed,' he said. 'It's a *stabilizing sherbet*.' He held the other one out to me. 'Go on. All travelling species must be *stabilized*. That includes the reptile.'

I watched as it changed from sky blue to volcano red before popping it into my mouth. Broccoli watched me nervously.

'It doesn't taste of anything,' I said, disappointed.

'Wait till you reach the pip,' said Secondus.

As I reached the centre of the sherbet, I realized that what I'd thought was a hard pip was, in fact, a thing of velvety, silky, soft goodness. I rolled it around with my tongue then bit into it.

A volcano of dizzying fizziness burst in my mouth. I whistled as it touched my throat and travelled from the top of my hair to the tips of my fingers, filling me with a roasty-toasty marshmallow-mushy feeling inside.

'It's AMAZING,' I gasped. 'Almost as good as my Tonic for Throbbing Toothaches, Toes and Thumbs.'

Broccoli watched me a moment longer. When I didn't melt or p°p, he put the sherbet into his mouth. 'You're right,' he said. 'It doesn't—' Before he could finish speaking, his face suddenly TWISTED.

'It *burns*,' he gulped, his cheeks turning a peculiar shade of grape. Beside him, Archibald's face was wrinkled in fizzy delight.

'Only if you bite it straight away,' said Secondus, unimpressed. He turned back to his clipboard. 'Now, where was *I*?'

I glanced at the sherbet machine. Now that Secondus was distracted, it was the perfect time for a quick investigation.

Without a sound, I crept towards it (super-stealth is a **MUST** skill for any **genius inventor**).

'I don't feel so good,' squeaked Broccoli. His eyes were watering, and his nose was producing a dangerous level of mucus.

'Neither The Office of Time, nor I, will be responsible for any side-effects or—'

BANG!

A fountain of stabilizing sherbets exploded into the air and scattered around me like RAINBOW-COLOURED HAILSTONES. I caught one and turned it over, the sherbet gleaming golden in the Perombulator light.

'It's brilliant,' I whispered.

'Get away from there!' yelped Secondus, darting towards me.

Hurriedly, I shoved the sherbet into my Inventor's Kit to investigate later. 'I was just looking,' I shrugged.

'Regulation 2,' said Secondus, glaring at me. 'Insignificants must <u>NOT</u> fiddle, touch or—'

Suddenly there was a loud *whirr* behind him.

'The Ripple Meter,' gasped Secondus.

'It's detected a ripple from the Cretaceous Age.'

I watched, eyes wide, as the butterfly slid upwards a notch.

'Mighty clocks! This is what happens when you travel through time without being properly stabilized,' hissed Secondus. He tapped the meter as if he were hoping to change it back again. 'Grand clocks! The Egyptians are building aeroplanes!'

'Is that all?' I scoffed. Talk about an overreaction.

'Is that all?' echoed Secondus shrilly. 'Is that all?! If we don't find your sister before this–' he jabbed the butterfly dial– 'reaches DOOM, the ripples will become permanent. IRREVERSIBLE! They could DESTROY all of reality as we know it!'

Ah. Maybe not an overreaction, then.

'All of reality?' whimpered Broccoli.

'That's not my fault,' I protested, glaring at the Ripple Meter. 'I told Nishi not to press that button.'

'I must get the time-landing coordinates from the Chief Finder and locate her before it's too late,' muttered Secondus. A line of worry had appeared on his forehead.

Without warning, the Perombulator shuddered violently.

'Thank the clocks,' said Secondus. He unclicked the Ripple

Meter from the Primary Console and slipped it into his pocket.

'Sit tight,' he said grimly. 'We're about to land.'

'N-N-N-O-O-O-T-T-T A-A-G-G-A-I-N,'

said Broccoli.

Archibald grinned, his cheeks flapping with delight.

We spun and swung sideways until we came to a juddering halt.

The sign above the door pinged from ACTIVE to STANDBY.

'Look lively, Insignificants,' said Secondus. He unplugged the Sat-Nav from the ship's wheel and strode to the door.

'We're here.'

Another Note From the Author about the Previous Chapter

Broccoli thinks that I have given you, the Reader, an OVERLOAD of information. I have told him that learning about time travel and Sat-Navs is not an OVERLOAD. If you were sitting beneath a herd of hippos that would be an OVERLOAD. However, I understand that you, the Reader, may want to take a break to: go to the toilet/ supply yourself with oxygen/feed a pet, sibling, parent or grandparent/check you aren't accidentally sitting under a herd of hippos etc.

When you are ready . . .

Lost and Forgotten

My jaw dropped to my feet and my eyes popped out on **GIANT** beanstalks.

This was the stuff of inventioning DREAMS

OF SPINGLY TINGLY MYSTERYDOM.

A moment to be remembered for—

'Uuuuuurggghhhhh,' groaned Broccoli behind me.

I sighed. Having an apprentice could sometimes be *very* hard work.

Secondus stuck a silver ticket on to the Perombulator door. Straightening his hat, he darted towards a signpost that was in the centre of the hallway in front of us. It was built like a tree with branches pointing in all directions. Attached to the trunk was a sign that read:

> WELCOME TO THE
> 72ND SATELLITE OFFICE
> OF T.O.O.T.
>
> (NOT HEADQUARTERS)

Next to the sign dangled a thick rope
labelled PLEASE PULL FOR ASSISTANCE. Secondus
gave it a tug. A moment later, an owl wearing a bowler
hat swooped down towards us.

WELCOME TO THE
72ⁿᵈ SATELLITE OFFICE
OF T.O.O.T.

(NOT HEADQUARTERS)

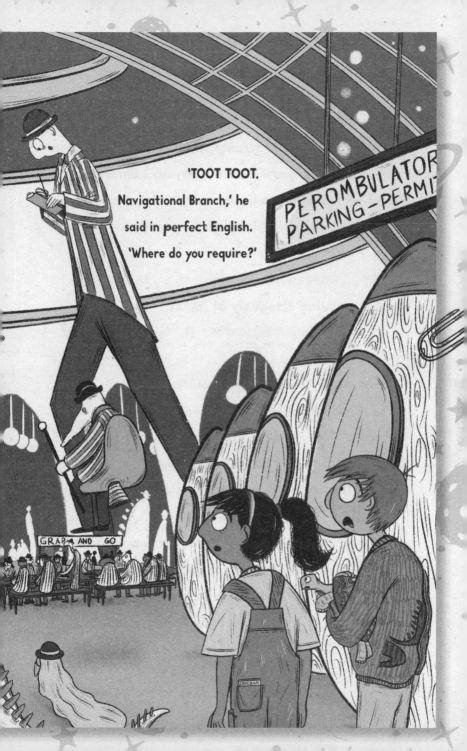

I goggled, my brain positively popping with bewilderment. Fortunately, the *Inventor's Handbook* had taught me how to stay cool in all kinds of strange situations. (If you've been reading carefully, you'll know this already.) *Unfortunately*, I hadn't yet taught Broccoli, who WHIMPERED and stepped back into the path of a slimy green creature.

'Hctaw erehw rey niklaw!' the creature shouted, pointing accusingly at its tail.
'Uoy tsomla dehsurc ti!'

'So s-s-orry,' stuttered Broccoli.

'Lost and Forgotten,' said the owl. It flapped its wings nervously. 'Take the fifth elevator at the end of the hall. Good luck. The Chief Finder's in a terrible temper. It's all that sniffing. The last one to visit came out in tears. TOOT TOOT.'

'TOOT TOOT.' Secondus tipped his hat and darted into the bustle of the hallway. 'Follow me, Insignificants.'

I hurried after him, my head spinning a full **360 degrees** as I looked around. The hall was ENORMOUS and bursting with noise. Officers darted in and out of doorways, bowler hats bouncing busily on their heads. The hats were different colours – red, green, purple, blue – each with different letters sewn on to the front.

The ceiling was built like a giant dome, and entirely transparent. Clusters of stars and glittering dust floated above us, flooding the hall with silvery light.

We wove past a long line of officers queuing outside a door labelled T.O.O.T. APPOINTMENTS. A couple of them nudged each other as we hurried past.

'Minor Insignificants,' said one. 'I had to take one to Headquarters once. He had the funniest-sounding name: Einstei—'

'Excuse me – pardon – EXCUSE ME,' piped an invisible voice as a tower of purple bowler hats swayed past us. 'Could you point me in the direction of Hatting – the ceremony for the MOOT officers is about to start. The Middle Officers of Time – that's right—'

'How – why – what *is* this place?' I spluttered.

I had so many questions buzzing around my brain that I was sure they were about to whizz out of my ears.

Archibald purred in delight, his mouth stretched into a wrinkly grin.

Broccoli looked a little green. Actually, a **LOT** green. Even greener than Archibald.

'Clear the way! Illegal time devices coming through!'
A uniform-wearing flamingo, pushing a trolley with several chained machines, darted between us and disappeared through a door marked CONTRABAND.

Broccoli gave me a worried glance.

'That's NOT going to happen to ours,' I whispered firmly. 'I won't let it.'

'**Beware the Guzzler!**' An officer with a yellow hat pushed a leaflet into my hand as we passed a stand marked INFORMATION. '2,450 TOOT officers guzzled already. All officers are reminded to upgrade their wormhole radars before travel! 2,450 guzzled alr—'

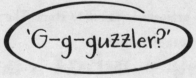

swallowed Broccoli.

Glimmers of light danced off the top of his head, making him look like an orange-topped avocado.

'I'm sure it's nothing to worry about,' I said.

Secondus snorted. 'Nothing to worry about? A Guzzler is every officer's **worst nightmare**. The most fearsome monster you hope NEVER to meet. One of the many reasons why you must never fall into a wormhole. Ever.'

'What's a w-w-wormhole?' whimpered Broccoli, pulling closer to me.

'You Minor Insignificants really don't know much, do you? Holes in space and time,' said Secondus. 'They're scattered all over **the Murkle**. The Perombulator systems don't work inside them so you definitely don't want to—'

Broccoli sneezed. Once. Twice. Three times.

This was NOT a good sign. The last thing I needed was for him to enter **FULL FRIGHT MODE**. Not when we had to find the time machine *and* stop Nishi destroying all of reality.

'Just think of Granny Bertha,' I interrupted loudly, shoving the leaflet into my pocket. 'Imagine what she would say to a place like this!'

'"Hold on to your hats",' murmured Broccoli. '"We've got some exploring to do."'

'Exactly!' I said.

'But I don't have a hat,' he sniffed.

Honestly. There's just *no winning* with some people.

'There,' declared Secondus, pointing to an elevator. 'Lost and Forgotten's that way.' He spurted forward, his chin set in determination. 'As soon as I have these coordinates,

I'll be able to find and **stabilize** your sister and stop her from creating More ripples.'

'What about *the Egyptians* and *the aeroplanes?*' I asked as we hurried past an archway labelled MAINTENANCE.

'Temporary ripples COLLAPSE once the person that created them has been stabilised and taken home, *so long as* they don't become **permanent**,' replied Secondus without turning round.

We were almost at the doors when a short, round man bobbed towards us. 'Secondus!' he shouted. 'Secondus Secondi! I thought it was you!'

'Mighty grand clocks,' muttered Secondus as he pressed a button to summon the lift. He smiled grimly and tipped his hat at the man. '**TOOT TOOT**, Professor Watts.'

Watts grabbed hold of his hand and shook it so hard that Secondus's hat bounced into the air.

'What are you doing here?'

'I'm on my **first mission**, Professor.'

'Grand clocks!' He squinted at his bowler hat. '**A**

New Officer of Time *already?* I still remember teaching you the Alpha Beta. Your father must be proud. How is Dayus?'

'He's—'

'I was hoping to talk to him about speaking at the next Academy Assembly.'

'That's—'

'What an officer!' he said. '**Untangled a Time Loop** with *nothing* but a DeMister. **Trapped** a Rampaging Cluster in the Milky Way.' He was shaking Secondus's hand with such ferocity I thought he was about to pull it right off.

The elevator doors opened. Broccoli hesitated, his nose twitching.

'*Go on*,' I said, and pushed him and his evil reptile inside before stepping in after them.

'More missions accomplished than any other officer. He'll be expecting **great** things from you!'

Secondus yanked his arm free. 'I really must be off, Professor.' He dived past him into the elevator, punching the floor buttons with haste. 'TOOT TOOT.'

'Are those Insignificants?' called Watts after us.

The doors HISSED shut.

'What was that about?' I asked.

'None of your tockwax,' said Secondus, hurriedly glancing at the Ripple Meter.

We *zoomed* downwards, the air whooshing through our ears until we clunked to a stop.

'Keep up, keep up,' said Secondus, dashing into a cobbled corridor lined with street lanterns.

'Watch out for Ti-Mite Tremors,' read Broccoli as we hurried past a sign nailed into the wall. 'Protection Advised,' he murmured, reading another. 'Continue At Your OWN RISK.' He sneezed and glanced around fearfully. 'What *are* Ti-Mites?'

As if in answer, there was a loud **THUMP** above us. The ceiling shook, the bricks rattled and the lights flickered. A moment later, thick chunks of rock dust hailed down from the ceiling.

Broccoli sneezed again and began hopping on the spot. 'I think it slid down my jumper – ooh, it tickles!'

Archibald rolled his eyes and tucked himself safely inside his shell.

'Here we are,' said Secondus, stopping in front of a

door. In the centre was a gleaming brass plaque that read: **Lost and Forgotten.** Underneath, in writing that was so tiny that I had to squint to read it were the words:

For the location, detection, identification and discovery of objects, persons, or other items which have been misplaced, lost or forgotten in time.

Another newer-looking plaque had been fixed below it:

SNIFFING
BY APPOINTMENT
ONLY.

Next to the first plaque was a brass knocker, about the size of my little finger.

'We don't have an appointment,' I pointed out, remembering the **ENORMOUS** queue upstairs.

Broccoli sneezed **again**.

Secondus frowned but said nothing. A loud whirring suddenly rang out from his pocket. His forehead wrinkled as he checked the Ripple Meter. '*Another* ripple. Sharks grow wings. They *fly*.'

'Sh-sh-sharks?' sniffed Broccoli, looking above his head.

'Sharks?' I echoed. This was a teensy-tiny bit worrying. Actually, very worrying. Imagine sending your apprentice to buy fizzpops only for them to get chomped instead. It would be an absolute TRAGEDY.

Secondus read the plaque again, then straightened his hat decisively. 'I can't wait for an appointment. I need these coordinates now.'

Taking a deep breath, he pounded the knocker against the door.

A deep, **belly-rumbling horn BLASTED** on the other side.

'Enter,' said a SHRILL voice.

The Chief Finder

On the other side of the door was the **biggest** room I'd ever seen. It was as high and wide as Mum's favourite football stadium. A purple carpet, lined with glowing lanterns, stretched out beneath our feet and disappeared into the distance.

On either side of us, from the floor to the ceiling, were shelves stacked with jars. **Big** jars, small jars, round jars, square jars, hexagonal, floating – jars EVERYWHERE. The shelves were labelled **FOUND PROPERTY**.

Automaton Arm

Tunnel Dragon Spit

GUZZLER Teeth

I whistled softly. 'Broccoli, I hope you're making notes. Don't forget it's your job to organize my – I mean – *our* – genius inventions. This is exactly what you—'

'Quickly, Insignificants!' interrupted Secondus, hurrying ahead. 'There's not a moment to lose!'

'WE KNOW,' I snapped, racing after him.

Ahead was an inconveniently **TALL** wooden desk. Its legs stretched from the floor and continued so high into the air that just looking at it made my neck hurt. At the very top of the desk, I could see a TINY figure sitting on a chair that was held in the air by a web of ropes.

There was another

 **THUMP** above us.

The shelves shook, the jars jiggled and a shower of dust sprinkled down from the ceiling.

A polished, melon-shaped mouthpiece whirred down towards us as we reached the desk. It stopped level with Secondus's face.

'State your business,' squawked a fearsome voice through the mouthpiece.

'I, Secondus Secondi—'

'Your business, not your name,' screeched the voice.

'We—'

'Quickly, boy, quickly. I don't have all the time in the world.'

'—have a Minor Insignificant lost in time,' spluttered Secondus.

There was a noise like someone sucking air through their teeth.

'Lost one, did you? How careless.'

'It wasn't—' Secondus caught himself and tipped his hat up and down nervously. 'I—'

'You may come up.'

The mouthpiece zipped upwards. A moment later, a rope ladder was thrown down to our feet.

'She wants us to CLIMB?' said Broccoli. He sneezed and stepped back. His eyes were dripping, and his nose was drizzling. 'No, no way. It's TOO high.'

'He suffers from vertigo too?' said Secondus, looking at Broccoli as if he'd never seen anything more **offensive** in his entire life.

I shrugged. 'Apprentices are hard to find.'

The mouthpiece whirred down again at top speed.

'Are you coming or not?' screeched the voice on the other end.

'On the way, Chief Finder,' sputtered Secondus, the mouthpiece zipping up before he'd even finished speaking. 'Stay here,' he said to Broccoli. 'Don't *wander off* and

DON'T TOUCH ANYTHING. Do you understand?'

'I'm not going anywhere,' said Broccoli, nodding furiously. He sat down beside the table leg and pulled out his copy of *Dinosaur World*. 'This is the latest edition. I still haven't had a chance to look at the free gift.' He waved an object at us. It was shaped like an enormous leaf, the tip sharp and pointed. 'It's an exact replica of a stegosaurus back plate. A scute! Isn't that amazing, Archie?'

Archibald made a disgusted KRRRR noise at the back of his throat and flopped his head down with a sigh.

(Drama queen.)

[A note from Broccoli: He is not.]

Secondus and I began our climb.

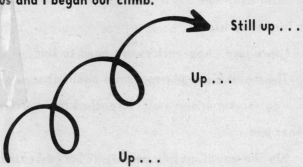

Still up . . .

Up . . .

Up . . .

Up we climbed . . .

Until Broccoli was a little orange-headed dot on the ground and Archibald was an even ~~eviller~~ tinier green smudge.

By the time I reached the top of the ladder, my hands

were aching and my breathing felt funny.

[A note from Broccoli: Granny Bertha is always telling me that lack of oxygen is a common problem at high altitudes. It is another reason I dislike heights.]

I dragged myself on to the desk and lay there without moving, absolutely sure that I must have been the first **inventor** in all of history who had climbed a desk the size of

Mount-STUPID-Everest!

'Couldn't you just build a lift?' I panted.

'The Chief Finder is known to dislike gadgets and gizmos,' said Secondus.

'Is she still alive?' screeched the voice I'd heard through the mouthpiece.

'She's quite alive,' said Secondus, hauling me up. 'Just delicate, that's all.'

Had I not been struggling to breathe at that very moment, I would have shown him exactly how DELICATE I really was.

As we got nearer, I saw that the owner of the voice was sat in a large nose-shaped throne.

She was the oldest-looking person I'd ever seen. Her face was more wrinkled than a prune, her eyes more grunkled than a gizzard. She was wearing a blue dress that puffed out round her waist like a ginormous balloon. Her hair was held in a tight bun on her head. Her nose was as straight as a ruler and the tip was purplish, like beetroot. She wore a pair of fearsome horn-rimmed glasses.

On the woman's shoulder was an even more ancient-looking pigeon. I'd never seen a sadder-looking creature in my entire life (not counting my DRONG of a sister). It was almost featherless and its eyes were pink and watery.

Secondus stopped in front of the throne, lifted his bowler hat a few centimetres off his head and put it back on again. 'TOOT TOOT, Chief Finder,' he said, his hat trembling a little. 'Thank you for seeing us.'

'Eh? What's that?' said the Chief Finder, holding a withered hand to her even more withered ear.

'I was hoping you'd be able to help us find—'

'Help you find?' she screeched. 'Do you see this?' Next to the throne was an enormous bowl overflowing with letters, objects and ribboned jars filled with pink tocks. 'I am the *Chief Finder*. Descendant of all the Chief Finders before me. My grandmother, Hortense – you might have heard of her –

oh, what a hooter she possessed. *Nobody like her* in all the Murkle! Found the **ENTIRE** lost city of **Atlantis** with one sniff. As for my mother, Sylvie, well – the Supreme Schnozzle is what we called her.' She clapped her hands and roared with croaking laughter.

'The Supreme Schnozzle.'

She stopped suddenly and squinted at me. 'A Minor Insignificant, eh? I haven't seen one of your lot since Agatha Christie wandered through a Time Crack. Fell directly into this office, she did. Quite the storyteller.'

'Chief Finder,' said Secondus.

'And who are you?' she said, moving her gaze to him.

'Secondus Secondi. A New Officer of Time. Chief Finder, I—'

'A Secondi, eh?' The Chief Finder squinted through her glasses. 'Ah, yes, you have your father's eyes. I met him when he was about your age. Many, many o'clocks ago.' She peered at him closely. 'I haven't met you before.'

'This is my first mission,' said Secondus, puffing himself to his full height. 'I—'

'I hear they're gifting him a new hat. A POOT, if I'm not mistaken.'

'POOT?' I sniggered.

'Perfect Officer of Time,' said the Chief Finder. She looked at me so fiercely that I took a step back. 'It is the highest honour.'

'Indeed it is,' beamed Secondus proudly. He straightened his hat. 'He's a credit to The Office of Time and I will be too. Which brings me to this.' He took out the vial of tocks from his pocket. 'Chief Finder, I am on—'

There was a thud above us. A cloud of dust rained on to our heads.

'On a—'

The Chief Finder held up a gnarled finger.

S-l-o-w-l-y - s-l-o-w enough to make a snail squirm – she took off her glasses. Then she lifted a TINY feather duster that was hanging round her neck and swept it across each lens.

She was the SLOWEST thing I'd ever seen.

Slower than:

① A slug
② A sleepy slug
③ A sleeping slug ○○○○○○○○○○○○○○

I jiggled my leg restlessly.

At **LAST**, she put her glasses back on.

'—on a Class Three emergency,' finished Secondus, barely able to hide his impatience. He waved the vial in the air. 'I need the time-landing coordinates from this time trail. *Please.*'

There was another **THUMP**. More dust rained on top of us. The Chief Finder took off her glasses and started cleaning them again.

'Daily discombobulation,' she grumbled. 'These Ti-Mites . . . poor Napoleon here has lost all his feathers thanks to them.'

The pigeon cooed sadly. She replaced her glasses then peered down at a dusty book in front of her. 'Strange, I can't seem to find you here. You do have an appointment?' she said.

Secondus hesitated. 'Well – no, not exactly.'

'No appointment?' The Chief Finder's eyebrows crackled upwards. 'Didn't you read the sign? No sniffing without one.'

'The Lost-in-time Protocol didn't—' Secondus cleared his throat. 'I was hoping you might be able to make an exception. This is a Class Three EMERGENCY.'

I groaned inside. Secondus really knew nothing about **The Art of Persuasion**. Even Broccoli could have done a better job than him.

[A note from Broccoli: I am, in fact, an excellent negotiator. Last Christmas, I persuaded Dad to play chequers instead of chess. It was a terribly exciting afternoon.]

'An exception?' screeched the Chief Finder. 'What did they teach you at the Academy? You must make an appointment through the proper channels like everyone else.'

Secondus took off his hat and put it back on again. 'But the Butterfly Ripples have already started.'

'Then I would advise you to hurry,' cackled the Chief Finder. 'What would your father say if you fail your first mission? You'd be the first Secondi to be sent back to the Academy. Fired, even.'

Secondus looked as if he were about to be SICK. 'But—'

'Good day to you both. Napoleon.'

With a great powdery kerflopple of wings, the pigeon flew towards the glass bowl, picked up a pair of pilot's goggles and went back towards the Chief Finder, wheezing for breath.

The Chief Finder lifted the goggles to her nose and sniffed gently. 'Earhart, eh?' she murmured. 'What are these doing in Zone -2?'

There was another **THUMP.**

More dust floated down on us.

The Chief Finder sighed, put down the goggles and

reached for her own dust-encrusted glasses.

That's when I had a BRAIN-WHIZZYING brain spark.

A moment of PURE, SIZZLING

 GENIUS.

'Wait,' I said. 'I might have something that can help.'
I whipped an object out of my pocket and waved it in front
of the Chief Finder's nose. 'Self-cleaning Specs!
Designed for long and short sightedness. Press the pink
button to change the eye power. The blue button to activate
the wipers.'

'A gadget, is it? No, thank you.'

'Oh, this is no gadget,' I said, taking a step towards her.
'This is a life-changing OPPORTUNITY.'

Napoleon swivelled his head and stared at me with one
watery eyeball.

'What are you doing?' hissed Secondus.

I cleared my throat loudly.

'Imagine,' I said, 'being able to continue your important
work uninterrupted. Imagine how much easier your life
would be if you didn't have to clean your glasses every time
you got dust on them.'

'Pardon her, Chief Finder,' said Secondus. 'She doesn't—'

'Let her speak, boy,' said the Chief Finder impatiently.

Secondus scowled and looked down at his shoes.

I took another step forward and looked up into those shrunken eyes. 'Don't you **deserve** better? These –' I held up the Self-cleaning Specs proudly – 'are the **VERY BEST**. Invented by my very own **genius hands**.'

[A note from Broccoli: With my help.]

'Self-cleaning you say?' said the Chief Finder.

'Why don't you try them?' I asked. 'If you do find them suitable – and I'm absolutely sure that you will – we could do a trade.' I leaned forward, ready to deliver my *ESHA NINJA BLOW*. 'You can keep the spectacles free of charge in exchange for giving us the coordinates we need.'

The Chief Finder blinked at me in formidable silence. Secondus opened his mouth as if he were about to say something, but thought better of it and shut it again.

With a loud creak, the Chief Finder leaned forward and held out her palm for the Self-cleaning Specs.

I held my breath as, s-l-o-w-l-y, she took off her own glasses and slid the spectacles on to her nose. Beside me, I could hear Secondus's hat wobbling nervously.

'It's the pink button for the eye power,' I reminded her. 'Blue to activate the wipers.'

'No, no, ah, yes, that is quite satisfactory,' said the Chief Finder, fiddling with the pink button. She peered at the two of us as if seeing us for the first time. Before she could say anything, there was a loud THUD. A cloud of white dust rained down from the ceiling.

The Chief Finder pressed the blue button. The wipers squeaked against the glass, forming two clear patches on the lens.

'It's wonderful,' said the Chief Finder, blinking. 'Quite, quite delightful.' She smiled, her face softening a little. 'In all my time of sniffing, nobody has ever offered me *anything* quite like this.'

I nudged Secondus. 'That is what you call **The Art of Persuasion**,' I whispered.

'I shall keep them,' said the Chief Finder. 'In exchange, I shall pardon your appointment. Just this once, you understand.'

Secondus blinked. 'You will?'

I wiggled my eyebrows at him.

'Thank you, Chief Finder,' he stuttered. He swept his hat off his head. 'I am most—'

'Napoleon!'

The pigeon flapped down towards Secondus, grabbed the vial in its beak and wheezed back towards the Chief Finder, dropping it into her outstretched palm.

The Chief Finder uncorked the vial and tapped the bottom lightly with a long finger. The tocks flew out, buzzing angrily, and disappeared above our heads in a shimmer of pink.

Holding the vial to her nose, the Chief Finder took a long, deep sniff.

'Hmm,' she said.

She took another even longer and more POWERFUL sniff than the first. I wobbled like a guitar string. Secondus's hat floated a couple of centimetres into the air and fell back on to his head.

She sniffed a third time.

This time, the sniff was so EAR-POPPINGLY LOUD that the shelves rattled, the desk dithered and the lightbulb trembled.

'Oh dear,' said the Chief Finder. 'Oh dear, oh dear.'

'What is it?' I asked, leaning forward. 'What can you smell?'

'Horsetails – that's a plant –' she said, then added, 'Fresh water, scales.' She paused. 'Yes, most definitely lizard scales. Bones, eggs and teeth – rather a lot of teeth.'

'And the Insignificant?' said Secondus. 'Can you smell her?'

The Chief Finder wrinkled her nose over the tube. 'Here we are. Rubber wellingtons, compass steel, sweat, spearmint.' Her nostrils flared. 'Wait, there's more.' She breathed in deeply. 'Ah, yes. A bicycle seat. An empty beans tin. Toasted canary feathers—'

'That's the time machine!' I said excitedly.

'Your Insignificant has landed in Zone -9,' said the Chief Finder. '-Z9-a1.1, to be precise.'

'-Z9-a1.1?' said Secondus. His eye twitched. 'Are you *sure?*'

The Chief Finder nodded. 'The smell of teeth is most distinctive. It's the enamel, you understand. It has an unmistakeable hint of blueberries.'

'O'clocks,' said Secondus. He took off his hat and put it back on again. 'Millions and millions of years and she had to land in that when.'

'*Which* when?'

'I've heard the climate is most pleasant,' said the Chief Finder, 'though I can't say the same for the local residents. The T-rex, *in particular*. And that's not to mention the star showers, of course.'

'Star showers?' squeaked Secondus.

'Oh, indeed,' said the Chief Finder. 'Zone -9 gets more star showers than *any* other time zone. Quite fascinating.'

Secondus swallowed. 'My grandfather got stuck in a star shower once. He was never the same after that.'

'Then I would advise you not to get stuck.'

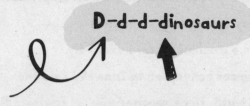

D-d-d-dinosaurs

With a *shriller-than-a-choking-mouse* squeak, the Perombulator came to a

SUDDEN
STOP.

'We're here,' declared Secondus. '-Z9-a1.1. The Cretaceous Age.'

Finally. Now I could find my DRONG of a sister and get ~~my~~ our time machine back. As for T.O.O.T. – well – I'd worry about them later.

With a loud groan, Broccoli peeled himself off the wall.

'I don't think I'll ever get used to this,' he moaned.

Archibald unstuck himself from the ceiling, landing

perfectly on his scaly feet. In stealthy silence, he took a couple of *surprisingly speedy* steps towards the door.

'It's moving again!' cried Secondus as the Ripple Meter clicked upwards. His eyes grew wide as he peered at the reading. 'Mighty clocks! Rabbits develop psychic powers.'

'R-r-rabbits?' squealed Broccoli.

I glared at the back of Archibald's shell.

There wasn't a PIPSQUEAKITY chance that I was going to let that tortoise **BEAT** me to an unknown world.

'There's not a moment to waste,' said Secondus, already spinning a lever on the Primary Console.

A screen above him flickered.

'*Perimeter check in progress,*' said a shrill, tinny voice.

With a SUPREME LEAP, I vaulted over Broccoli's evil reptile and raced to the door.

'Wait an o'clock,' cried Secondus. 'The perimeter check isn't—'

I pulled the door open and came face to face with . . .

OK, I'm JOKING.

I didn't come face to face with a T-rex (not at that particular moment anyway).

Broccoli has told me that authors should not joke with their readers. I have reminded him (again) that this is MY journal and I can make jokes if I want to. I have also pointed out that it is important to spring unexpected surprises on your readers to make sure they are PAYING ATTENTION.

What I actually saw when I opened the door was

a world of breathtaking beauty.

Stretching out in front of me, for miles and miles, was the most enormous forest I had EVER seen. The trees bulged out of the ground like swollen cucumbers. Above us, the sky was light pink, the clouds shimmering with streaks of silvery-blue. The air was hotter than I had expected; I could feel it pressing on my face, warm and earthy and sweet. And the noise! It was as if I'd stepped into a prehistoric concert. From all over, I could hear buzzing and rumbling, every sound magnified so loudly that I could feel the vibrations in my bones.

Everything was so brilliantly beautiful that just looking at it made my brain EXPLODE like the fireworks at Diwali.

There was a sniff over my shoulder.

'It's wonderful,' whispered Broccoli. 'Look, Archie,' he said, holding the tortoise in front of him.

Archibald snickered, his face twisted in an expression that looked like he was thinking 'at long last'. With fierce determination, he stuck his head out of his shell and flapped his front feet as if he were trying to take off.

'This is where your ancestors are from,' said Broccoli. 'I wish Granny and Archimedes could see—' He gasped suddenly, his lip quivering. 'Why . . . is the ground . . . *d-d-down there?*' he stuttered, pointing.

I peered over the edge of the Perombulator and realized two things:

① I had been so busy admiring this unknown world that I had ignored what was right in front of me.

② What was right in front of me was **AIR**. Lots and lots of air.

There was a loud beeping behind me. *'Perimeter check – inconclusive. Manual check recommended.'*

'Secondus?' I asked.

'Mighty clocks!' he cursed behind us. 'There's something **wrong** with the eyescope. This view just doesn't look right.'

'That might be because we're not on the ground.'

'Not on the ground?' He snorted. 'What are you talking about?'

'I mean the ground is down **THERE.**' I pointed to the earth a **long** way below us. 'And we're up **HERE.**'

'Impossible,' he said, darting towards us. 'Time-landing coordinates are triple-checked for safe landing. There's no way we would have — O'clocks . . .' He trailed off as he caught sight of the ground below.

Suddenly, there was a **LOUD** chomping noise beside us. I glanced at Archibald who responded with a "well it's not me" look. Secondus craned his neck round the side of the Perombulator and breathed in sharply.

'O'clocks,' he said again. Without another word, he sprinted back to the eyescope. 'O'clocks, o'clocks,' he muttered as he twisted it round. 'We've landed on top of it.'

'On top of **what?**' I asked.

Secondus ignored me and darted towards the Sat-Nav, scowling. 'This didn't come up in our Perombulator exams.'

Holding on to the doorframe, I leaned out of the Perombulator. My breath caught in my throat. Without a word, I grabbed hold of Broccoli and pulled him forward.

There, beside us, was a

REAL, breathing
DINOSAUR.

Its skin was a wrinkly greenish-brown and covered with hundreds of bristly hairs. Its neck was thick and wide, like a truck, and gloriously long, rising upwards in a perfect smooth arc. Its head was a peculiar oblong shape, with a perfectly round bump on the top. Beside the dinosaur was an even taller tree, its branches gleaming with fiery-coloured leaves. As we watched, the dinosaur raised its head and tore them off, chewing them slowly with a loud **SHLUP-SHLUP** noise.

Broccoli whimpered and stepped so close to me that he trod on my toe.

'It's a d-d-d-d . . .' he whispered.

'I don't understand,' muttered Secondus.

'D-d-d-d . . .' said Broccoli.

'I entered the right coordinates.'

'D-d-d-d . . .' repeated Broccoli.

I slapped him on the back.

'Dinosaur,' he breathed, his eyes shining with excitement. 'It's a dinosaur.'

'Isn't it amazing?' I grinned.

I, Esha Verma, **genius inventor extraordinaire**, was the first inventor in all of prehistory **and beyond** to see a **DINOSAUR** with my very own eyeballs.

It was the BEST moment of my ENTIRE life.

Even better than:

1. Winning SECOND place in the Young Inventor of the Year competition for the first time.

2. Watching Nishi be cut in half at the fair (until they put her back together).

3. Finding out that Mum had finally agreed to let me have a real pet (OK, that might have been a dream).

It was for moments like this that I had invented ~~my~~ our time machine in the first place. Like all the inventors before me (or after, depending which way you were looking at it), I, Esha Verma, would transform people's lives with my creation.

I could see it ALREADY.

An entire corporation of Time-travelling Tours.

All the most important people in the world queuing up outside my door just to have a whizz in ~~my~~ our time machine.

An army of apprentices.

All I needed to do was FIND the time machine ~~(and my DRONG of a sister)~~ and persuade T.O.O.T. Headquarters that they should let me keep it.

(There was also the *slight* problem of Butterfly Ripples, but I was absolutely certain I could invent my own kind of stabilizing sherbet to neutralize those. Especially now I had one to investigate.)

'How are we getting down?' I asked, turning round. 'Can't you just zap us to the ground?'

'The Perombulator is **NOT** designed for zapping,' said Secondus impatiently. 'I need coordinates to land safely.' He looked up from the Sat-Nav and cleared his throat awkwardly. 'Besides, we have *another* problem. We've landed on the wrong continent.'

'The wrong continent?' I raised a puzzled eyebrow. 'But you had the time-landing coordinates.'

'When travelling beyond Zone -5, the Sat-Nav must be recalibrated to account for interference.'

I raised my other eyebrow. 'So?'

'So I was busy checking the Ripple Meter when we left.'

'You didn't recalibrate it?' I couldn't believe my **GENIUS ears.**

'We are in the correct when, just not the correct where,' retorted Secondus. He was scowling so fiercely that he looked as if he'd swallowed a lemon. 'I've recalibrated it now. We should be on the move shortly.'

I put my hands on my hips and gave him my best *ESHA LASER GLARE.* 'How shortly? Because the time machine — and, of course, my sister — are still out there —

and we can't get to either of them while we're on the back of a – a—'

'Pelorosaurus,' declared Broccoli. I turned round to find him sketching frantically in his notebook. 'Did you know that "pelorosaurus" means "monstrous lizard"? But that's only because of their size. They're actually **herbivorous**.'

I goggled at him. We were on the **WRONG** ←
CONTINENT and he was drawing dinosaurs?

'You don't need to remind me of the urgency,' snapped Secondus indignantly.

The Perombulator wobbled suddenly.

Secondus leapt towards the eyescope. 'O'clocks! It's **turning round!**' he hissed.

'Granny and Archimedes will never believe this,' murmured Broccoli as he continued scribbling.

'Can't you take us to another when?' I interrupted impatiently.

'Not whilst the Sat-Nav is recalibrating,' said Secondus. His hat twitched like a fretful flea. 'Until it's finished, we're stuck.'

The Perombulator jiggled.

'But what about the time machine—' I began, but I didn't finish because at that moment the Perombulator wobbled again, throwing us **back** towards the Primary Console. The door flung shut as we rolled along the pelorosaurus's body, slowly at first then a little faster, faster still – until the Perombulator whizzed downwards like a bowling ball and landed with a **THUMP** on the ground.

'Well, that wasn't so bad,' said Secondus in a muffled voice. Bobbing upwards, he squinted through the eyescope. 'O'clocks,' he said. 'That looks like a dinosaur foot—'

Something hit the Perombulator.

Something **BIG** and **STRONG**.

Something so **BIG** and **STRONG** that it sent us zinging through the air like a dandelion in the wind. **CRASH!** We bounced– once, twice, three times– before being flung out of the Perombulator door . . . through the air . . . on to the **massive** leaves of a tree.

The Small Beak Lizard

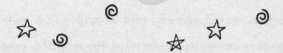

Down we whizzed, slipping and sliding until we hit the earth with a **THUD-THUMP-CRASH.**

'Ow,' I groaned.

'O'clocks,' moaned Secondus.

'Archie?' snivelled Broccoli.

Head still spinning, I stood up, the world SWAYING a little around me. We had landed inside an enormous bush. On either side were huge purple leaves that dangled over us like colossal sponges. Each one oozed with a buttery sap, which dripped to the earth with a soft glubby sound.

'I – hate – this – time – zone,' muttered Secondus, smacking a blob off his bowler hat. 'It's even worse than I expected.'

The air was hot down here and sticky. I could feel it clinging to my arms and face like glue.

I lifted my shoe and goggled at the ground, my inventor's instincts shivering in realization. 'We're

standing on PRE-HISTORIC EARTH,' I murmured.
Closing my eyes, I took a deep breath so that I
would remember this exact feeling. After all,
when I became a famous inventor, people would ask me—

'Archie?' squealed Broccoli. He dropped to his hands and
knees. 'Where are you?'

I sighed. 'I'm trying to have a **MOMENT** here.'

'Can you both be quiet?' HISSED Secondus, peering
through the bush. 'Something might hear you.'

Past his shoulder, I could see more plants and trees. An
enormous yellow insect suddenly buzzed above our heads.
As it reached a tree, something long and stringy shot out
from the branches and snatched it out of the air. The
branches rustled for a moment, then there was a **LOUD**
crunching noise. I swallowed and slipped my fingers over
the **Extend-a-Hand**.

Just in case.

'Thank the clocks the Perombulator is the right way up,' said
Secondus. The machine had landed upright a short distance away
from us. He slid his hat back on to his head, wincing as a glob of
sap dribbled down his cheek. 'We should wait inside until the Sat-
Nav finishes recalibrating. There's no knowing what nefarious—'

'I can't see Archie!' gabbled Broccoli, leaping up. He sneezed. 'We have to find him!'

'He's probably still inside the Perombulator,' I said without batting an eyelid. 'That tortoise knows how to look after himself.'

Just then, there was a **LOUD** rustling noise ahead of us. I tightened my grip on the **Extend-a-Hand**.

A moment later, a dinosaur appeared through the trees.

It was the strangest-looking creature I'd ever seen. Its ears extended out of its forehead in two violet-coloured bony lumps. It had a small orange beak and a large candy-floss-coloured flap of skin dangling from its chin. Its eyes were black and its body was almost entirely covered in fur. It blinked, its gaze pausing on the Perombulator.

'O'clocks!' gasped Secondus.

Broccoli appeared to have FROZEN with shock, his snot suspended like an icicle.

The dinosaur took a step forward, then paused, squinting at the Perombulator.

'Mighty clocks!' hissed Secondus, checking his pockets frantically. 'My *Dinosaur Directory* is still in the Perombulator!'

The dinosaur took another step forward.

'Broccoli, what *is* that?' I asked.

His lips twitched, but no sound came out.

The dinosaur continued to stare at the Perombulator. I prodded Broccoli gently. He gasped, his snot swaying back to life. 'It's a Berthasaurus,' he whispered, his voice hoarse.

I goggled at him.

He wasn't SERIOUS.

[A note from Broccoli: That was hardly the moment for a joke.]

'**A Bertha – what?**' began Secondus.

'Berthasaurus,' whispered Broccoli. 'The small beak lizard. Carnivorous.'

'It's going to see us,' whispered Secondus.

'Not through these bushes,' said Broccoli. 'The Berthasaurus has terrible eyesight and smell, but its hearing is excellent. We'll be safe as long as we stay quiet.'

'How can you be sure?' said Secondus uncertainly.

'That's what Granny told me.'

'*Granny?*' echoed Secondus.

'My apprentice knows every reptilian fact there is to know about dinosaurs,' I hissed fiercely. 'More than your *Dinosaur Directory* ever could. Now be quiet.'

With slow, awkward movements, the Berthasaurus moved

towards the Perombulator. It was over double our height and walked on two long legs, waddling clumsily across the ground.

Secondus stiffened as the Berthasaurus reached the Perombulator. It tapped the side of the machine with its beak. The Perombulator wobbled so hard that it **BOPPED** the Berthasaurus right back.

The dinosaur squawked and leapt backwards, tripping and falling on to the ground. It was like watching Dad dance.

'Archie,' gasped Broccoli suddenly.

That's when I spotted him.

The tortoise was a short distance behind the Berthasaurus.

The dinosaur lumbered up and eyed the Perombulator suspiciously before poking it and leaping backwards again – narrowly missing Archibald.

'It's going to squash him,' I murmured.

That's when Broccoli did something very un-Broccoli-like.

He stepped **OUT** of the bush towards the Berthasaurus, which had its back to us.

'Broccoli,' I whispered.

'What, in the name of o'clocks, is he doing?' hissed Secondus.

I **goggled** at my apparently-not-so-timid apprentice as he crept towards Archibald.

Screeching noisily, the Berthasaurus continued to

investigate the Perombulator, too distracted to notice the tiny human coming towards it.

I watched in trembling silence, absolutely certain that I was one wrong step away from losing my apprentice because of his **VILLAIN** of a pet.

Broccoli was almost next to Archibald now. One arm outstretched, he leaned forward and grabbed hold of his shell.

With a **LOUD** screech, the Berthasaurus leapt on top of the Perombulator. Secondus *winced*.

Ever so slowly, Broccoli took a step back.

At that moment the Sat-Nav let out a shrill whirring noise.

The Berthasaurus snapped round, its eyes scanning the bushes. Broccoli froze, his hand still clasped round Archibald's shell.

'Switch it off,' I hissed.

'I can't,' said Secondus, jabbing at the device. 'It's automated.'

The Berthasaurus squawked and jumped off the Perombulator, squinting in our direction.

Broccoli stayed *absolutely still*.

With a mighty squawk, the Berthasaurus scooted forward, moving past Broccoli,

 **TOWARDS US.**

Dizzying Doughnuts

My mouth **dropped**.

'Broccoli was right,' I said. 'It really does have bad eyesight.'

'O'clocks,' gasped Secondus. He whipped out his clipboard. 'There must be a protocol for this!'

'Don't you have a weapon – a dinosaur dart or something?'

'**A weapon?** What kind of asteroid head do you think I am? Section 2, Regulation 2.9 of Proper Office Etiquette: nobody should carry a weapon at any time, to prevent any adverse or regrettable ripples.'

The Berthasaurus scurried closer, its beak glinting in the sunlight.

I clenched the **Extend-a-Hand** and dug my other hand into my Inventor's Kit.

'Here it is!' gabbled Secondus, waving his clipboard. 'Dinosaur Protocol: escape immediately.'

I snorted incredulously. 'Well, *that's* helpful.'

The Sat-Nav whirred even louder, then clicked into silence.

With a confused squawk, the Berthasaurus stopped a few paces away from us, its eyes searching the leaves. It was close now, close enough for me to smell its reptilian odour, warm and foul like rotten eggs.

I held my breath.

Beside me, Secondus shut his eyes, his hat trembling a little.

The Berthasaurus trilled curiously, its head tilted in the air. It stayed in this position for a few moments. At last, with a slow shuffle, it turned away.

'RECALIBRATION COMPLETE,' declared the Sat-Nav loudly.

With a triumphant screech, the Berthasaurus swivelled back towards us, beak outstretched.

OH. NO.

'O'clocks!' cried Secondus, his hat shooting a few centimetres off his head. The Berthasaurus dived towards us with incredible speed – I was sure this was the end of our ADVENTURE . . . until—

'Over here!' shouted a voice.

My mouth dropped as I saw my snot-nosed apprentice leap into life. The dinosaur screeched to a halt and snapped round, narrowing its eyes at the tiny leaky thing jumping in front of it. Broccoli waved one hand in the air, the other firmly gripped round an irritated Archibald.

'Leave them alone!' he shouted, his voice quivering, his snot leaping about like a rabbit on springs.

'What – in the name of o'clocks – is he doing?' breathed Secondus.

'Distracting and diverting,' I said, rummaging frantically in my Inventor's Kit. 'A very important skill for apprentices. Essential for buying time in difficult situations.'

'Time for what?'

'For genius plans.'

'Over here!' cried Broccoli again, his voice shrill with fear. The Berthasaurus let out a dangerous screech.

'These will do!' I pulled out a paper bag containing three iced hard-as-mountain-rock doughnuts.

'What are those?' said Secondus incredulously.

'Dizzying Doughnuts. The first prototype.'

'Doughnuts?' His eye twitched. 'What are you going to do? Thrash it with toothache? Sweet-talk it to surrender?'

I decided to ignore him. After all, not everyone can think like an **inventor**.

At that moment, the Berthasaurus threw back

its head and ejected a **GIANT** globule of scarlet **spit** from its mouth.

It flew across the air, narrowly missing a **stunned** Broccoli, and landed on the earth with a scorching hiss.

'O'clocks.' Secondus threw himself flat on the ground. 'This never came up in Archaeological Studies!'

'I didn't know dinosaurs could do that,' I said, open-mouthed. With a mighty squeal, the Berthasaurus leapt after Broccoli, who turned and raced towards the Perombulator.

I clicked my **Extend-a-Hand** to the Long-distance-throw Function, aimed the doughnut at the Berthasaurus and fired. It zipped through the air in a mighty sweet swoop and landed a few paces ahead of it.

I held my breath and waited, my inventor's instincts tingling with excitement.

The Berthasaurus charged across the doughnut without so much as a dither.

'It didn't work!' squealed Secondus unhelpfully.

'Must've been a dud doughnut,' I pointed out.

'A dud do—' he blustered, his words disappearing into a thin squeak.

The Berthasaurus launched another **GIANT** ball of spit at Broccoli. With surprising

acrobatics,

Broccoli leapt sideways, the spit landing millimetres from his leg, where it immediately formed a sticky, steaming, scarlet glue.

'What will Father say?' stuttered Secondus. 'My first mission and we're going to be sizzled.'

'I haven't travelled through the Murkle to become dinner for a dinosaur!' I snapped. 'Now will you STOP flapping?'

I loaded another doughnut into the **Extend-a-Hand** and threw it. It fell a few paces ahead of Broccoli and

EXPLODED, just like I wanted, releasing a peach-coloured puff of dizzying vapour.

Had Broccoli not been so busy staring at the Berthasaurus, he might have seen it.

Instead, he ran right into it.

[A note from Broccoli: Had Esha aimed the doughnut, I wouldn't have become a target in the first place.]

I watched, **open-mouthed**, as Broccoli suddenly stopped and spun on the spot, a silly smile across his face.

'Did you see that?' I said. 'It WORKED! It actually worked.'

(I mean, obviously it did.)

'What are you talking about?' retorted Secondus wildly. 'You missed.'

I'd been so **HOPPINGLY EXCITED** to see my invention in action that I'd forgotten all about the Berthasaurus, which was still barrelling towards Broccoli.

'**Broccoli, get out of there!**' I shouted.

Broccoli tottered on his feet like a breeze-blown beansprout.

The Berthasaurus flip-flapped towards him, its beak outstretched.

'Oh no, you don't,' I said, loading another doughnut into the **Extend-a-Hand**.

'Nobody eats my apprentice. Especially NOT furry fossils.'

The doughnut zipped through the air and exploded in front of the Berthasaurus's face with another burst of peachy-coloured fumes. It reared upwards with a surprised squeal and spun on the spot.

'Got you!' I shouted. 'Eat doughnut, you creepy crawler!' I punched Secondus on the arm. 'Wasn't that **brilliant?**'

'Brilliant?' spluttered Secondus shrilly. His hat wobbled with indignation. 'Brilliance is following regulations. Brilliance is getting a **POOT** hat like my father. Brilliance is *not* firing doughnuts at a dinosaur.'

Suddenly the Berthasaurus stopped spinning, its arms frozen in the air.

A **DEEP** belly-gurgle sounded from within its body.

'What have you done?' gasped Secondus, open-mouthed.

I took a step back.

The Berthasaurus twisted as if there were something inside it that was about to **EXPLODE**. Then, without warning, it let out the

biggest BURP

I had ever heard.

It was a **BELCHER**.

A GALE-FORCE WIND.

An AIR BOMB of such MIGHTY PROPORTIONS that it catapulted the ~~Burpasaurus~~ Berthasaurus into the air.

I watched, spellbound, as it **WHIZZED** high above our heads, squealing like a runaway train.

'On your feet!' shouted Secondus. Holding his hat, he leapt out of the bushes. '**This is our chance!**'

We sprinted forward, the Berthasaurus flip-flapping above us.

'Secondus, watch out!' I yelled. '**It's coming back!**'

The Berthasaurus hurtled downwards like a large hailstone, its legs wiggling frantically.

I grabbed hold of Broccoli and leapt out of the way as it landed with a COLOSSAL

CRASH.

Birds and insects exploded into the air. My teeth rattled. Broccoli sneezed.

'Mighty grand clocks,' groaned Secondus. 'The Academy never prepared us for anything like—' He stopped, his face twisting in panic as he touched his head. 'Where's my—?'

'Here.' I pulled his now flat-as-a-chapati hat out from under me and tossed it over. Secondus stared at it in horror. Before he could say anything, the Berthasaurus let out a high-pitched squeal. A moment later, there was a **deep rumbling** noise.

'That sounds like feet,' I said, my stomach quivering.

'Evidence shows that the Berthasaurus probably moved in herds,' mumbled Broccoli, still dazed. 'Granny and Archimedes are still investigating.'

I goggled at him. 'You're telling us that NOW?'

'Inside the Perombulator,' said Secondus, leaping upwards as the trees started to shake. **'MOVE!'**

The ground trembled beneath us as we sprinted towards the Perombulator. Never in all my inventioning life had I run as **LIGHTNING FAST** as I did at that moment.

Glancing back, I saw a handful of Berthasauruses emerge from the trees, their eyes turning in our direction.

'O mighty grand clocks,' panted Secondus.

With a SOPRANO of SQUAWKS, the Berthasauruses reared their heads.

Three steps –

two steps –

one –

A burst of scarlet exploded into the air just as we reached the Perombulator. Wrenching open the door, Secondus pushed us inside and leapt through after us, only just managing to slam it shut before it was hit by a thundersome volley of Berthasaurus spit.

On the Move (again)

'O'clocks,' spluttered Secondus. 'Why couldn't my first mission have been the Olmecs? The Mughals?' He shoved the Sat-Nav into the ship's wheel. The Perombulator whirred. 'All of the Murkle and it had to be **DINOSAURS!**'

'Hurry up!' I cried, pressing my face against the window. 'They're coming!' The Berthasauruses were moving closer, ready to launch another shower of sizzling spit.

'They must make it in their chin flaps,' said Broccoli, peering through the window beside me. 'Granny wondered why they had those.'

Before I could tell him that now was not the time to be thinking about fossil functions, the Perombulator hummed louder. The walls shook violently. The Berthasauruses hesitated, squinting at the machine. A moment later, there was a thunderous thrumming, then the Berthasauruses vanished from view.

'O mighty clocks!' shouted Secondus, his face bright with triumph. 'I did it!'

'Did what exactly?' I snorted. 'Those were *my* Dizzying Doughnuts. And Broccoli fought the Berthasaurus.'

'I did?' said Broccoli, horrified.

Archibald made a noise that sounded like 'should have let me at it'.

'Sort of. Not really . . . but you *did* distract it. It was the best distracting and diverting I have ever seen.'

Broccoli blinked. 'Really?'

'If you hadn't, I wouldn't have come up with my all-important **genius plan** that saved us all.'

'I suppose not,' said Broccoli uncertainly.

Secondus made a face. **'Genius plan?** I was the one that got us out of there. I wish Father could have seen that! He'll never believe it. And I didn't even have my *Dinosaur Directory*!'

'I **can't believe** I saw a real Berthasaurus,' said Broccoli, slumping back against the wall. He still looked a little queasy from the Dizzying Doughnut.

Archibald rolled his eyes and tucked his head back into his shell.

Honestly, reptiles are all the same.

A few moments later, we shuddered to a halt.

Taking a large lungful of air, Secondus blew

into his hat, puffing it back into shape, and squashed it on to his head. 'The right when and where,' he announced. He darted to the Primary Console and twisted a lever, his hat wobbling at top speed.

'*Perimeter check – in progress,*' said the tinny voice.

The Primary Console pinged. A scroll whizzed out of the top of a rusty cauldron labelled FORECAST and smacked Broccoli on the nose.

'OW!' he squealed.

I snatched it up, my eyes darting across the parchment.

> **WARNING:**
> **STAR SHOWER EXPECTED**
> **AT NIGHTFALL.**
> Risk to Perombulator systems: HIGH.
> Officers advised to leave
> AS SOON AS POSSIBLE to avoid—

'Give me that!' said Secondus. He scowled as he read it then shoved the parchment into a pipe where it disappeared with a loud schlup.

'Is this what the Chief Finder was talking about?' I asked, my inventioning instincts tingling with warning. 'Could it destroy the time machine?'

'Possibly,' said Secondus. He jabbed a few buttons. A stabilizing sherbet shot out of the Primary Console. He slipped it into a paper bag and put it into his pocket.

'*Sherbet* to stabilize your sister – check.'

'Possibly?' I echoed. I hadn't travelled all the way to **PRE-FLIPPING-HISTORY** and battled a Berthasaurus just for a star shower to sizzle the time machine. I could already imagine my DRONG of a sister looking up at the sky while the time machine **COMBUSTED** beside her.

'But we'll find it before then,' said Secondus, moving with new urgency. 'No star shower is going to leave *me* stranded!'

'STRANDED?' I said sharply.

Broccoli sneezed. 'Stranded?' he whimpered.

Archibald looked up with interest.

'Stuck - trapped - **MAROONED,**' said Secondus, his face grim.

'We know what it *means*,' I said impatiently.

'Star showers can last for months,' said Secondus. 'There's no going in or out of one when it starts.' He grabbed a book titled *Dinosaur Directory* from the shelf above his head. 'That means we need to be *quick*. We **won't**

survive in this era. We get out before the star shower, or not at all. Do you understand?' he continued, talking to us as if we were a pair of **IGNORAMUSES**. He shoved the book into his pocket and stood a little straighter. 'We find and stabilize your sister, then you deactivate the time machine so I can impound it –'

Broccoli glanced at me, his nose twitching as if he were about to sneeze. I folded my arms and gave him my best "everything is under control" look.

'– by tonight.'

The Primary Console crackled. *'Perimeter check – complete. No immediate perils detected.'*

'Finally!' said Secondus. He unclicked the Ripple Meter and darted to the door. 'Follow me, Insignificants!'

A blueberry-smelling breeze tickled our faces as we raced outside. We had landed on a **ginormous** hill. The sky was orange, the clouds speckled with purple and pink. In the distance, I could see another forest sprouting out of the ground.

Broccoli nudged me. 'Esha.' Not far away from us the ground had a large dip in the

middle. Inside the dip were spatters of honey-coloured goop. 'Nishi must've landed there.'

But there was **NO**

PIPSQUEAKITY SIGN

of **THE TIME MACHINE**

OR my **DRONG** of a sister now.

'Just wait till I find her,' I **growled**.

'There!' cried Secondus suddenly. His hat twitched with excitement as he waved yet another strange-looking device at us. It was made of glass and sealed on both ends with golden stoppers. Inside was a cloudy liquid containing three green bubbles. A tiny spinner whirred on the top. On the side were the words **SPECIES TRACKER**. 'Do you see?' he said, jabbing at the device. 'She's only one mile away!'

'**One mile?**' SQUEAKED Broccoli.

'One mile?' I *groaned*.

An important note about **genius inventors**: we are *far*

too busy running our **genius** brains to worry about actual running around.

That is a job for apprentices.

Unless, of course, we're running from parents, teachers or DRONGS of sisters.

'Can't you move us closer?' I asked hopefully.

'I've told you already,' said Secondus in exasperation. 'I can't land the Perombulator without coordinates. It would be like throwing yourself off a Casimir slide without a timechute.'

'That doesn't sound good,' sniffed Broccoli.

'A Casimir *what?*' I demanded impatiently. 'And have you ever thought about *improving* your Perombulator's design? Because I think—'

But Secondus had **ANNOYINGLY** already darted forward, his hat dancing with determination. 'Almost there, Insignificants! Wait till I tell my father that I've finished my first mission. A "Lost in Time" too!'

Attack

Down the hill we went
racing over the bumpy earth
until we were quite hot
and bothered and STILL not at the bottom.

We must have been about halfway when we heard a LOUD
FLAPPING in the air behind us. I didn't even need to
turn round to know that it was MORE dinosaurs. That's
what you call an **inventor's** instinct.

'O'clocks,' gulped Secondus. He scrabbled in his pocket
and pulled out his *Dinosaur Directory*, flicking hurriedly
through the pages. A small pack of greyish-brown dinosaurs
with huge wings and heads built like long swords were
flying in our direction. 'Not this one, not this one—'

'Pterodactyls,' breathed Broccoli.

'Pterodactyls?' echoed Secondus. His hat quivered as
he looked up at them. **'O'CLOCKS.'**

'What do—' I began.

'Their **bones** are filled with air like bird bones,' said Broccoli, pulling out his notebook.

'Fascinating, but what do—'

'My father fought one of these,' whispered Secondus. 'Nearly took off his finger!'

'In fact, people used to think that birds were descended from **pterodactyls**, but that's not true,' gabbled Broccoli with super speed. 'Birds are *actually* descended from theropods—'

'BROCCOLI!' I hissed. 'What do **pterodactyls** eat?'

'Fish, crabs, insects and other animals. They're **100% CARNIVOROUS**.'

The **pterodactyls** were almost above us now, flying in a diamond shape with military precision, **KAW-KAWING** to each other as they approached.

'What about their eyesight?'

'Oh, it's excellent,' said Broccoli. 'They've probably already seen . . . us.' His face suddenly paled as he realized what he'd said. 'Maybe I should have mentioned that first.'

'You don't say,' I growled.

[A note from Broccoli: It's difficult to remember everything when you're faced with creatures of such magnificence.]

We watched as the first **pterodactyl** of the group swivelled its head towards us. With a **HEART-PIERCING KAW-KAW**, it slowed to a sudden halt, hovering patiently in the air. The others did the same. Each and every pair of **pterodactyl** eyes locked on to us like missiles on a target.

We looked right back at them – GIRL (and others) VS DINOSAUR – in the most **EPIC** EYE CONTEST the world has ever known. (Fortunately, I had a lot of practice with epic eye contests thanks to my DRONG of a sister.)

'We have to get back to the Perombulator,' whispered Secondus. 'We'll be safe inside.'

'Broccoli, what do you thi—' I began.

Before I could finish, Secondus unhelpfully stepped backwards. As he put his foot down, the **pterodactyl** at the front let out a shrill **KAW-KAW** and **DIVE-BOMBED** towards us.

'BACK TO THE PEROMBULATOR!' shouted Secondus.

'This way!' I said, grabbing Broccoli, who was about to run full speed in the opposite direction.

We HURTLED up the hill, the **kaw-kawing** of the **pterodactyls** growing **louder** and **louder**.

'We'll **NEVER** outrun them,' shrieked Broccoli, a shell-shocked Archibald bouncing in his hand. 'They're too fast!'

'JUST KEEP MOVING!' shouted Secondus, racing in front of us.

I could feel the beating of wings behind me as the **pterodactyls** drew closer . . .

I could hear their shrill **KAW-KAWING** as they called to one another . . .

We were almost (miraculously) at the Perombulator when, out of the corner of my eye, I saw Broccoli turn to look back — and **TRIP.**

He went headlong into the dirt. He was down just long enough for the leading **pterodactyl** to swoop in and grab his leg in its sharp claws.

'Esha!' squealed Broccoli as he rose, upside down, into the air.

With a **HEROIC LEAP**, I, Esha Verma, forgot all about the danger to myself and **dived towards** my drippy apprentice. (Well, I didn't want to train another one, did I?) Dodging Broccoli's sneezes, I grabbed hold of his hands. The **pterodactyl** screeched in outrage and flapped its wings, trying to pull itself clear. But I was holding on now and NOTHING in this reptile realm was going to make me let go.

'He's MY apprentice,' I shrieked. 'Find your own!'

With an angry **KAW-KAW**, the **pterodactyl** released him and we tumbled back down. Pulling Broccoli to his feet, I shoved him towards the Perombulator.

'QUICKLY!' roared Secondus, who was already in the doorway. He took off his hat and threw it at the **pterodactyls**. It whizzed through the air, catching them by surprise.

They pulled up into the sky with a **KAW-KAW;** the hat whizzed back to Secondus like a boomerang. 'That's for my father!' he shouted.

I CHARGED for the door.

But I'd only taken a few steps when something sharp took hold of my dungarees and

LIFTED ME INTO THE

AIR. ←

'Get off me!' I yelled, kicking and flailing. 'I **DEMAND** that you put me down this INSTANT.'

'LEAVE HER ALONE!' shouted Broccoli at the **pterodactyl**.

It made a vicious **KAW-KAWING** noise. Although I didn't understand PTERODACTA-LINGO, I was almost certain it was laughing.

'ESHAAAAAAA!' cried Broccoli again. The other

pterodactyls **KAW-KAWED** hungrily at the sound and dived down to the Perombulator while I dangled from their leader's claws.

'Mighty grand clocks!' cried Secondus. He grabbed hold of Broccoli and yanked him into the Perombulator, clanking the door shut behind them.

'SECONDUS!' I bellowed, wrestling with the **pterodactyl's** legs as it rose higher into the air.

'OPEN THAT DOOR RIGHT NOW! SECONDUS - ARE YOU LISTENIN–'

KAW - KAW!

With a triumphant SCREECH, my captor flew around in a circle, and towards the forest, carrying me away with it.

An Unexpected Flight

(Only to be read after you have recovered
from Secondus' RUDE behaviour)

I am absolutely sure that you, the Reader, must be thinking that being carried away by a **pterodactyl** is a MUST experience for anyone visiting the Cretaceous Age. It is not. It is, in fact, about as fun as:

1. Swimming in a swamp of starving piranhas.
2. Playing piggy-in-the-middle with a pair of GIRAFFES.
3. Cleaning out Mister E's cage.
4. Watching the football with **Mum**.
5. Watching the football with **Dad**.
6. Watching the football with **Mum** and **Dad**.
7. Holidays with my DRONG of a sister.
   (Clue: Not fun at all.)

Had I not been a **GENIUS INVENTOR**, I'm sure that I would have screamed/cried for help/wriggled like a helpless worm.

[A note from Broccoli: I am quite sure that Esha did all of these things.]

OK, so maybe I hadn't needed to ESCAPE from a **flying pterodactyl** before, but **genius inventors** have to be ready to deal with all kinds of jams and pickles. Which was why I never travelled anywhere without a spoon.

Or a fork.

Or a spork.

As we soared higher into the sky, I decided that neither a spoon/fork/spork was going to be much help in my present predicament. Not unless I could trade it for my freedom and, judging by the way I was being carried AGAINST MY WILL, I was absolutely sure that even **The Art of Persuasion** wasn't going to help me at this particular moment.

If there was one positive angle about my situation, it was that I was only dealing with

<u>ONE</u> pterodactyl.

[A note from Broccoli: That's because the others were more interested in getting their teeth into us.]

As per my speedy calculations, there were exactly three

courses of action I could take:

① Psychically wish myself somewhere else.

② Wait and see what happens (Dad's favourite).

③ Escape.

From experience, I knew that Option 1 would almost certainly never work. I tried it anyway. Nothing. Not even a piddling pulse of psychic possibility.

I moved onto Option 2 and ran through everything I knew about **pterodactyls**:

① They ate meat.

② **I** was meat (*Definitely*. Without a doubt).

③ Their bones were filled with air (UNHELPFUL).

I looked up at the **pterodactyl** to try to figure out how hungry it looked. Unfortunately, from the angle at which I was hanging, it was impossible to tell if the **pterodactyl** planned to eat me. Of course, there was always the *chance* that it did not want to eat me at all. Maybe it didn't think I was a two-legged takeaway. Maybe it was just giving me a welcome tour of its neighbourhood.

But it was a very slim maybe. Slimmer than the skinniest slice of salami. Probably best not to chance it.

That left me with Option 3:

ESCAPE.

I looked down and **immediately** wished I hadn't.
Far below my legs, I could see an entire forest of green.
An entire forest of green that looked a little too FAR
AWAY for comfort.

I didn't need to be a health-and-safety expert to know
that jumping from this height would probably (absolutely)
NOT be a good idea.

So I continued to dangle and wondered how it was that
a **genius inventor** such as myself could end up in this
unexpected situation (clue: blame **SECONDUS**) when, in
the far distance, I spotted a river twisting between the
trees. Now you, the Reader, may well be thinking that I
should have been trying to escape instead of admiring the
scenery, but you are forgetting that I, Esha Verma, am a

genius inventor extraordinaire and I'm always twenty steps ahead of everyone else (except giants and basketball players who have very long legs).

The moment I saw that river I was hit by

an IDEA.

It was an idea of such awesomeness that it was a pity nobody was there to witness it. This is another reason why inventors need apprentices.

As the **pterodactyl** continued whizzing onwards, I concocted my **MASTER PLAN**.

It had three simple steps:

1. Unstick myself from the **pterodactyl's** claws.
2. Fall into the water.
3. Congratulate myself on SURVIVING.

I was *almost sure* that falling into the water from this height wouldn't **kill** me. I was MORE sure that the **pterodactyl** was going to **EAT ME**, so it was a risk I was willing to take.

On we flew, closer and closer to the river, until I could see the water glittering just ahead of me. Ever so slowly — slow enough so that the **pterodactyl** wouldn't notice what I was up to — I poked around my pocket and pulled out my

INSTA DE-STICKER SPRAY.

[Broccoli is wondering why I didn't use my **Extend-a-Hand** to free myself from the claws of this rude creature. I have told him that, at that moment, my inventioning risk assessment told me that the INSTA DE-STICKER SPRAY was the best course of action. I've also told him that the next time he is being carried in the claws of a **pterodactyl** he is free to try both inventions and see which one works for HIM.]

As we passed above the river,
I squeezed the INSTA DE-STICKER
SPRAY on to the **pterodactyl's** claws.

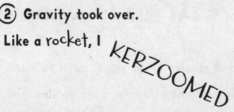

Two things happened at once:

① The spray worked.

(OBVIOUSLY. Did you think it *wouldn't?*)

② Gravity took over.

Like a rocket, I KERZOOMED

down . . .

down . . .

down . . .

towards the river where I landed with an

ENORMOUS

S P L A S H.

Meanwhile . . .

A note from Broccoli:

Esha has given me permission to describe what happened to Secondus and me while she was being carried away by a pterodactyl, so that you, the Reader, have a better idea of the Big Picture.

She has also pointed out that my storytelling talents are no match for her own and that I should be careful not to bore you, the Reader, in case you throw away this book and do not find out what happens in the end. So:

The Sorry Story of What Befell James Bertha Darwin after he was snatched from his time and taken hostage in the Cretaceous Age.

It began on a day like any other. I woke up and gave Archibald his breakfast. For any of you who plan on keeping a tortoise, I have found that the most nutritious breakfast is a bowl of lettuce leaves—

Esha has interrupted to tell me that the reader has ALREADY fallen asleep.

What happened to Broccoli

(written mostly by Broccoli)

'They took her,' I said, staring at the door of the Perombulator.
'They took my amazingly brilliant genius teacher.'

[A note from Broccoli: I most definitely did not say that.]

Outside, the pterodactyls were still trying to break through the door.
I could hear the thundering of their wings, their claws scratching, their
shrill **KAW-KAW** as they screeched to each other.

My nose twitched the way it always does when it senses danger.

The dials on the Primary Console whirled frantically.

'Hostile species detected. Hostile–'

'Flapling fossils,' hissed Secondus as he rushed towards the console. 'My
first mission and I couldn't even keep hold of an Insignificant. What would
Father say?' His face was shiny with sweat, his hat trembling like a leaf.

He pulled a lever on the Primary Console. A yellow light flashed
across the board, followed by an automated voice saying, '*Deterrent
Mode engaged*.'

'What's the deterrent mode?' I sniffed, stepping back from the
Primary Console. 'It doesn't sound very safe.'

As if in answer, the Perombulator started to shake.

'This should scare them away,' said Secondus grimly, dusting off his hat.

A pterodactyl smacked against one of the windows.

'*Dinosaur World* didn't mention this in their pterodactyls edition,' I whimpered, grabbing the rail. 'I didn't think pterodactyls would be so . . . well – *vicious*.'

Archibald bobbed his head in sorrowful agreement.

'**Father warned me about them,**' said Secondus, putting his hat back on. He shook his head with annoyance. 'I should have been more careful!'

The Perombulator juddered faster, the floor and ceiling quivering with the force of its movement. The Primary Console flashed, throwing beams of light through the windows. A bell clanged so loudly that it felt as if it were tearing the air apart. Archibald's poor little head shot back into his shell.

With my hands clutched round the rail, I staggered to another window to look for Esha. The pterodactyls hovered in the air, watching the Perombulator warily, but there was no sign of her.

Archibald poked his head out and touched his claw against my palm. 'I know, Archie,' I whispered. 'We have to find her.'

Suddenly a pterodactyl flew towards the windowpane, striking it fiercely with its beak. I tumbled back in fright, the eye of the pterodactyl following me hungrily.

'Are you sure the Deterrent Mode is working?' I asked,

my nose wobbling in panic. The pterodactyl was looking at me as if I were the most delicious thing it had ever seen.

Another pterodactyl hit the door.

'Hostile species detected. Evasive action recommended.'

'Gizzle-brained Guzzlers!' hissed Secondus. He shot over to the window as another pterodactyl smacked against it. 'They're even worse than Father described!'

'I don't suppose you can move us back to when we landed?' I sniffed, desperately trying to hold back a sneeze. 'We could wait inside the Perombulator until the pterodactyls have flown past—'

'And risk a Time Coil?' cried Secondus incredulously. 'Do you want our **brains** bubbled and our knees knuckled? The Perombulator Deterrent Mode is supposed to work! Professor Beebus told us that—'

'Hostile species detected. Evasive action—'

The Perombulator shook sideways like a see-saw. At that moment, there was a fearsome scraping noise above our heads.

'Reptilian rascals!' exclaimed Secondus. 'They're on the roof!'

I looked down to see Archibald quaking in his shell.

[A note from Esha: I am quite sure that Archibald was probably shaking with laughter.]

'I won't let them eat you, Archie,' I said, looking him in the eye. 'I promised Granny Bertha that I'd look after you. You're safe with me.'

'We have to activate the roof repulsion!' Secondus darted to the Primary Console, his hat bouncing like a spring.

'AAAHH—'

I couldn't hold it any longer.

'AAAAAHH—'

Where was that tissue?

'AAAAHHHCHOOO!'

With a sequence of shrill **KAW-KAWS**, the Perombulator tipped dangerously forward . . .

and T O P P L E D . . .

'Warning,' declared an automated voice through the ringing of the bell. 'Perombulator *unstable*.'

and T U M B L E D . . .

'Warning: Perombulator *unstable*. Deterrent Mode disengaged.'

It rolled and spun us around - tortoise and apprentice - like clothes in a washing machine until we landed with a painful thump. I groaned. Why was travelling in time so *bumpy*?

'Blasted boneheads!' muttered Secondus.

'Warning: Perombulator *unstable*. Deterrent Mode dis—' The voice clicked off only to be replaced by another. 'Warning: Perombulator upside down—'

'Secondus?' I said, wobbling to my feet. My nose quivered. There was no sign of him anywhere.

'Here,' said a voice above my head.

I looked up. Secondus was wrapped round the ship's wheel like an octopus, his hat still, miraculously, on his head.

Outside, there was the sharp **KAW-KAW** of a pterodactyl bouncing against the Perombulator door.

'They're not giving up!' I cried, holding tightly on to Archibald.

A red light flashed on the Primary Console. 'Perombulator upside down. Door lock compromised. Warning—' Something pinged off it and smacked against the wall.

'Grand clocks!' cursed Secondus, whipping back his hand as the Primary Console let out a jet of orange smoke. The Ripple Meter whirred and clicked upwards. 'Geese become the new rulers of Imperial China!'

'Geese?'

I sneezed again.

'There's not a moment to waste!' cried Secondus. 'We have to turn ourselves THE RIGHT WAY UP! Prepare yourself!'

'For what?' I yelled over the noise.

'A TIME SPIN,' bellowed Secondus.

'WARNING - Perombulator upside down. Door lock compromised.'

'How do I do that? I don't know anything about Time Spins!' There was another smack against the door. 'And what about Esha and her sister?' I cried fiercely. 'We can't leave them!'

'We're not going to be able to find them if the pterodactyls eat us,' snapped Secondus. He clanked a lever. 'Triple speed - check.'

THUMP.

The door trembled.

'Secondus . . .' I whimpered, pressing myself against the wall. Never mind dinosaurs and adventioning. I just wanted to be back home in my favourite chair.

There was the sharp BRING-BRING of a telephone.

'Incoming call,' said a voice from the Primary Console. 'Father.'

'O'clocks,' cried Secondus, his voice a thin squeak. 'O'clocks, o'clocks.'

Dangling dangerously in the air, he picked up the receiver of an old-fashioned telephone.

THUMP THUMP.

'TOOT TOOT, Father,' he shouted. Another pterodactyl smacked against the door. 'Yes, Father, the mission is going extremely well - a "Lost in Time" - there's some zonal interference, Father - I remember everything you've taught me - can you hear me? - Mighty clocks!' He slammed the phone down and jabbed a sequence of buttons. 'No Secondi has ever been fired—'

THUMP! THUMP! THUMP!

'They're in attack formation!' I squealed as one pterodactyl after another dived at the door. It shook violently, creaking under the strain.

'—or eaten by a pterodactyl! What will Father say?'

'Couldn't you ask him for help?' I asked shrilly.

'Ask for help?' shouted Secondus, his hat quivering with indignation. 'I am a Secondi. We don't need help!'

'*Time Spin Protocol selected. Warning: Risk of FLATTENING, JAMMING OR EXPLOSION. Proceed?*'

THUMP! THUMP!

Secondus punched another button.

'*Time Spin initiated.*'

The Perombulator rumbled and rattled.

'*Door lock compromised. Warning—*'

THUMP.

The sign above the door pinged from **STANDBY** to **ACTIVE**.

Archibald tucked his head back into his shell. I wished I could do the same.

'Here we go!' shouted Secondus. He gripped the ship's wheel, his hat shaking. 'Hold on, Insignificant! This won't take long!'

THUMP!

THUMP!

There was the sound of wood splintering. A cacophony of shrieks echoed outside. The Perombulator trembled with such ferocity that I could hear my teeth chattering.

'WHAT'S HAPPENING?' I wailed, sneezing again.

'Time Pressures!' bellowed Secondus.

A pterodactyl rapped the window viciously with its beak.

'They'll rock the navigation systems like a tock on

B-O-N-G-O-S!'

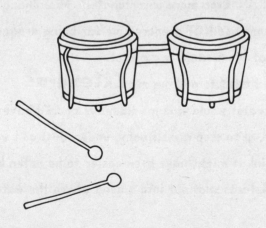

A Knotty Situation

While Broccoli and Secondus were **abandoning** me, I was trying not to be swept away by a river, which was A LOT faster-moving than it had looked from above.

[A note from Broccoli: I was not abandoning Esha. I would never do that. Even if I wanted to, I could not. The Apprentice-Inventor Agreement forbids it.]

Fortunately, I could no longer hear the **KAW-KAW** of the **pterodactyl,** so I was sort-of-almost sure that I'd left it behind. Unfortunately, I'd lost my INSTA DE-STICKER SPRAY. Even more unfortunately, Miss Zhang's swimming lessons had **NOT** prepared me for being dragged along a river at the speed of a rocket.

Every time I tried to pull out my **Extend-a-Hand,** the water would spin me sideways and I'd have to flip-flap-flop to stop myself going under. Just as I was starting to think it might have been easier to be eaten by a **pterodactyl,** I was spat out into a bend where the water slowed.

Keeping a lookout for the pesky **pterodactyl**, I whipped out my **Extend-a-Hand** and aimed it at a colossal tree root on the riverbank.

BRIZZZINNNNNNNNG!

I pulled myself on to the earth and

BLEUURGGGHHHHHHHH...

out came all the water I'd swallowed.

Had the pesky **pterodactyl** (or any other dinosaur, for that matter) decided to turn up at that very moment, I would almost probably have been **EATEN** and the world would have faced a tragic future without my **genius inventions.**

But you, the Reader, have nothing to fear FOR THAT DID NOT HAPPEN. ⟵

Once my insides had finally stopped bouncing like a blancmange, I squelched to my feet and assessed my situation.

WHAT I KNEW

WHAT I DID NOT KNOW (yet)

- I was wet . . .
- I was lost . . .
- Nishi and ~~my~~ our time machine were in the forest . . .

- Where I was . . .
- How to find Broccoli and Secondus . . .
- The exact whereabouts of Nishi and my time machine . . .

There was also the teensy-tiny problem of Secondus deactivating the time machine and me being in trouble with T.O.O.T., but there is only so much a genius brain can worry about at once. No matter which way you looked at it, it was a knotty situation.

Fortunately, the *Inventor's Handbook* had three simple instructions on untangling yourself from knotty situations. *Unfortunately*, I couldn't quite remember them at that particular moment. Before I could remind myself, there was a **THUNDER-RUMBLING ROAR.** I decided that the best thing at that moment was to put as much distance between myself and the roar as possible . . .

The *Inventor's Handbook* would have to wait.

~~An Unfortunate~~ The WORST Unfortunate Incident Ever

I ran, charging under dripping ferns and spiky bushes.

ROAR!

The noise rolled across the entire forest.

I ran faster, trying not to think about **hungry stomachs** and **SHARP TEETH** and DRONGs of sisters when . . .

THUDUMP . . .

I tripped and sailed forward, my *Inventor's Handbook* (and a few other things) tumbling out of my pocket as I spun through the air, landing with a soft **PLOP** . . .

on a

GIGANTIC PILE
OF

DINOSAUR

 # POOP.

It was a **MONUMENT** of **MUCK**.
A FORTRESS of **FOULNESS**.

And the **SMELL!** It was the pongiest stench my nostrils had **ever** sniffed. *Worse* than the rotten fish I'd accidentally left in Dad's sock. *Worse* than the bag of freeze-dried vomit that had exploded in the freezer. *Even worse* than Nishi's toxic wellingtons!

Holding my breath, I slid down and landed with a soft SHLUP on the ground.

As I squelched to my feet, I realized two things:

1. Fortunately, the **THUNDER-RUMBLING ROAR** had stopped.
2. Unfortunately, dinosaur poop was the stinkiest, stickiest sludge I'd ever encountered and it was ALL OVER ME.

Now you, the Reader, may be thinking this was the Worst Unfortunate Incident Ever.

Wrong.

It was about to get **much worse**.

Because, as I tried shaking off the sticky, stinky poop, I heard a noise in the ferns ahead of me. I froze, my heart thumping, as a **dinosaur** came through the leaves. It was about my height with a stone-coloured fin on top of its bald head. It had feathered arms with sharp talons and a long, pointed tail.

The dinosaur tilted its head and cooed as it caught sight of me. Its eyes were a fiery orange and clever-looking. I held my breath and wished that Broccoli was with me so that I would know exactly what this dinosaur was (and, most importantly, what it **ate**).

[A note from Broccoli: I am still not entirely sure what dinosaur Esha encountered. It is quite possible that she met a species that has not yet been discovered by palaeontologists. I have tried calling Granny Bertha to ask if she knows. Unfortunately, she is still in the middle of the Amazon.]

The dinosaur took a step towards me and sniffed the air. I wondered if I had enough time to draw out my **Extend-**

a-Hand before it decided to pounce. The dinosaur sniffed the air again. Its face wrinkled in disgust. To my astonishment (and relief), it turned away from me, but then bent down towards my *Inventor's Handbook*. With a sharp trill, it IMPOLITELY ran a long purple tongue over the open page.

'Do you mind?' I said, forgetting all about the fact that this dinosaur could probably eat me if it wanted. 'That's a FIRST edition.'

The dinosaur glanced at me with a devilish look in its eyes. It was the same way Nishi looked at me when she was about to be a complete DRONG.

Before I could move, the dinosaur grabbed the book in its greedy talons and **DISAPPEARED** into the trees.

'**OI!**' I yelled. Quickly, I scooped up the other things that had fallen out of my Inventor's Kit and chased after the dinosaur.

'GIVE IT BACK!'

[A note from Broccoli: For anyone planning to travel to the Cretaceous Age, I would advise you to run AWAY from a dinosaur, not towards it.]

Unfortunately, running after a dinosaur is hard work.

It is even harder when the dinosaur moves like a MACHINE. As I huffed and puffed after it, this reptilian robber powered through the trees until, with an annoyingly graceful leap, it hurdled over another pile of poop and vanished.

'I'M TALKING TO YOU!' I panted as I swerved round the dung. 'That's MY handbook!' As I came out on the other side, I spotted the dinosaur a short way ahead of me.

A hair-curling screech rang out in the distance. The dinosaur stopped suddenly, head raised, listening. I charged forward, fingers hovering on the BOPPER function of the **Extend-a-Hand**. After all, my FIRST EDITION INVENTOR'S HANDBOOK was at stake. No way was I going to let it go without a fight. There was another screech. A second later, another bald-headed dinosaur appeared through the trees. I stopped as I saw the object dangling from its jaws.

The object was purple and hideous and covered in yellow umbrellas.

My heart dropped.

It couldn't be.

With an evil screech, the **SECOND** dinosaur dropped the hideous purple thing and tried to snatch my *Inventor's*

Handbook from the first. With lightning speed, its thieving twin ducked out of reach and leapt away with a victory shriek. The second stared at the hideous purple thing for a moment then ran after the first dinosaur, disappearing into the trees.

Forgetting all about my *Inventor's Handbook*, I hurried forward, crossing my fingers and toes in the hope that I was somehow wrong for the first time in my **genius** life.

There, on the ground, where the dinosaur had left it, was one of Nishi's wellingtons. The front half, including Nimbus Dewey's signature, had been completely chewed off; the rest was covered in a thick glob of dinosaur spit.

A **DOOMING FEELING** rose from the tips of my toes to the ends of my hair. Nishi loved these wellingtons. They were as important to her as my *Inventor's Handbook* was to me. She would never let a dinosaur take one **unless**...

I looked at the chomped wellington, feeling a little sick inside.

OK, so Nishi was a DRONG. And she'd pressed The Big Red Button on the time machine even when I'd specifically told her not to. And she absolutely didn't understand the magic of inventioning. But she was still my sister. I hadn't *really* wanted her to get eaten by a dinosaur. And I absolutely hadn't thought that I wouldn't see her again.

If Nishi had been eaten . . .

Who would I wrestle on the sofa for the remote?

Who would I make faces at behind Aunty Usha's back?

Who would I race to the kitchen when Mum was frying pakoras?

Most importantly, who would I blame when my inventioning prototypes did not quite work as expected?

pakoras

And how would I explain this UNFORTUNATE INCIDENT to Mum and Dad? Time machine or no time machine, they'd ban me from inventioning for **ETERNITY** once they discovered Nishi had been **DINO-GESTED**.

This was **worse** than being in trouble with **T.O.O.T.**

Worse than almost being spuzzled by a Berthasaurus and dino-napped by a ~~pterodactyl~~. **EVEN WORSE** than being ROBBED of my FIRST EDITION *Inventor's Handbook.*

In fact, I decided, as I stared at the Nishi-less wellington, Nishi being eaten was, without a dither of a doubt,

The WORST

Unfortunate Incident Ever.

Note From The Author

Broccoli has just interrupted me to say that now would be a good time for you, the Reader, to take a break so that you don't drown yourself in a puddle of tears. He is looking quite **WET-EYED** himself, so I have agreed, mainly so that he doesn't drip all over this journal.

Go on.

Shoo.

Skedaddle.

Vamoose.

Oh! Back so soon?

Now, are you sure you're ready?

Quite sure?

Absolutely?

Then you may read on.

(But do remember that I will not be responsible for any further **gloom, desolation or despair** you may experience from this point onwards) . . .

News Today

19TH JULY 1841

UNIDENTIFIED FLYING OBJECT FRIGHTENS FOWL

Residents in Dartmoor were stunned yesterday when a peculiar egg-shaped object appeared in the sky above them. The object is believed to have remained in the air for a few seconds before disappearing.

James Fork, farmer and witness to this spectacle, said, 'It was an alien spaceship – I just know it! I saw one of them staring at us through the windows. Looked just like a tortoise. Frightened the feathers off all my chickens! I'll be lucky if they ever lay an egg again.'

The police have said that investigations into the appearance of this object are still ongoing.

After The **WORST** Unfortunate Incident Ever...

I had **THREE** options:

① Howl in despair (like you, the Reader).

② Find Secondus and Broccoli.

③ Invent a way for Broccoli and Secondus to find me.

I knew from experience that Option 1 did **NOT** do anything except give you a sore throat and stinging eyes (so I absolutely did **NOT** do this).

[A note from Broccoli: I am quite sure that's not true.]

Unfortunately, I absolutely did not feel like inventing. This was very **PECULIAR.** I had never, ever not felt like inventing before, but it's very hard to think of **genius inventions** when a **dinosaur** has **EATEN** your one and only sibling.

In fact, at that moment, I wasn't even worrying about the time machine or being in trouble with T.O.O.T. All I could think about was if there were any way to get Nishi **BACK.** Secondus would know — I was sure of it. I just had to find him.

There was just one teensy-tiny problem.

I had no idea how to get back to the Perombulator.

On every side of me was forest. Lots and lots of forest. The trees were TALL and stretched into the air like old, knobbly fingers. Plants grew around them in all directions. Some spread across the ground like enormous cobwebs; others were wide and smooth like upside down peppers. There was so much forest that it was impossible to see where it began and where it ended.

I took out a slightly melted fizzpop and sucked it between my teeth so I could think. A blue insect, about the size of a large cat, chirruped noisily above my head. As I watched it disappear into the branches, I was hit by a single, zinging BRAIN SPARK.

Based on my genius calculations, there was no way that I could see the Perombulator from the ground, but if I could climb up high enough . . .

After a quick inventor-level inspection, I picked a tree with branches that were thicker and hung lower than the others. Using my **Extend-a-Hand**, I pulled one of the branches towards me, testing it against my weight. Once I was happy that I wouldn't become an inventor PANCAKE, I swung myself towards the tree and wrapped my legs round the trunk. At that moment, the Earth began **shaking**.

A tornado of tremors trembled through the tree, into the branches, rattling my eyes in their sockets and my teeth in their gums.

Along with the shaking came a **THUNDER-RUMBLING ROAR** that I recognized instantly. It was the same **THUNDER-RUMBLING ROAR** that I'd heard by the river.

My inventor's instincts tingled to

RED ALERT.

I let go of the branch, landing with a painful **THUMP** on the ground. I could see the entire forest shuddering behind me as something **ENORMOUS** stampeded through the trees.

Shoving my **Extend-a-Hand** back into my pocket, I RAN like a rocket on ultra-quick jets, branches snap-cracking behind me, the **ROAR** growing louder, until I hurtled into a clearing, where I saw, by a prehistoric miracle, or maybe thanks to the inventing gods, the opening of a cave almost completely hidden by a curtain of leaves, an opening too small for a dinosaur (hopefully), but just perfect for a HUMAN.

The Time Spin:
The Second Attempt

The Cave

I slithered through the entrance, only just scrambling inside before I heard it.

The **shudder** of heavy footsteps.

THUMP! THUMP! THUMP! THUMP!

ROAR!

If I had not been a **genius inventor**, I'm absolutely sure I would've become a puddle on the spot. Instead, ignoring my trembling inventor's instincts, I, Esha Verma, bravely peeped through the curtain of leaves.

There, in the middle of the clearing, was the
DON OF ALL DINOSAURS.
The **LEADER** of **LIZARDS.**
The **FIERCEST** of **FOSSILS.**

A living, breathing,

TYRANNOSAURUS
REX.

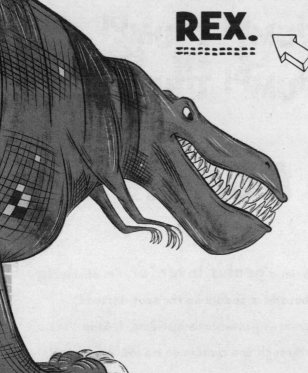

It towered as TALL as a

DOUBLE-DECKER BUS.

Its legs were as **THICK** as

TREE
TRUNKS.

Its mouth was filled with a **skin-tingling army** of

COLOSSAL TEETH

that shone like swords in the sunlight. With each step,
it sent a quiver through the ground, its tail crack-
snapping like a whip. The air around it **STANK** of rotten
meat and old boots.

Holding my breath, I pressed myself against the wall of the cave and thought about how **UNFAIR** it would be if I, too, were eaten by a **PONGY LIZARD**. If only I'd stopped Nishi pushing the button on the time machine, none of this would have happened.

The T-rex's eyes blinked across the clearing, vicious, alert and unmistakeably *hungry*. It lumbered forward, sniffing the air.

I was still plastered in dinosaur dung so I was absolutely sure that it wouldn't be able to smell me. But, just in case, I shut my mouth, pinched my nose and closed my eyes, trying to stop any possible **DELICIOUS HUMAN MEAT** smell from reaching its too-big nostrils.

The T-rex sniffed again. The sniff was so powerful that I felt myself being LIFTED OFF THE GROUND.

I must have hovered in the air for a few seconds when, far away, something screeched. The T-rex let out another **THUNDER-RUMBLING ROAR**, dropping me back to earth. There was the loud **THUMP-THUMP** of its feet moving away. I remained where I was, my heart thudding, until I was absolutely sure that it was gone.

Slowly, I wobbled to my feet and thanked the inventing

gods and dinosaur droppings for my lucky escape.

THEN . . .

something rustled at the back of the cave.

I froze.

NOT ANOTHER DINOSAUR.

I squinted into the darkness, but it was impossible to see anything.

I thought about switching on my headtorch so that I could see whatever IT was, but then IT would be able to see me too. Instead, I pulled out my **Extend-a-Hand**, my finger on the READY FOR BATTLE button.

I'd just about had enough of these vile, villainous reptiles. No way was I going to be chomped up by whatever was lurking in the cave.

Not when I'd just survived becoming tea for a **T-rex**.

A **dirty, two-legged creature** shuffled out of the shadows, its fists raised in the air.

The creature goggled at me.

I goggled at the creature.

Why You Should Never Trust a DRONG

'Esha?'

'Nishi?'

Without thinking, I dropped my **Extend-a-Hand** and pulled my sister into a hug.

'You're alive!' I squeaked.

'You're here!' she said, squeezing me so tightly that I could hardly hear her.

'That dinosaur—'
'— don't believe—'
'— your wellington—'
'— been here for ages—'
'I thought I'd never—'
'— see you again,' she finished.

I'm still not entirely sure what made me hug my **DRONG** of a sister, but fortunately, at that moment, my **GENIUS BRAIN** realized what I was doing.

Nishi's peanut brain must have kicked in at the same time because we both stopped grinning at each other and blinked as if we'd come out of a mystical spell.

'Anyway,' said Nishi, pushing me away, 'you **STINK.**'

'Not as **bad** as *you*,' I said. I picked up the **Extend-a-Hand** and switched on my headtorch. Nishi looked **terrible**. Her hair was sticking up like an electrified bird's nest and she was plastered in leaves and dirt. All I could see of her face were her eyes, which shone like two large moons. They looked slightly wet.

'Have you been *crying?*' I asked.

'No,' she snapped a little too quickly.

I looked down at her feet. On one foot she was wearing a wellington; on the other she was wearing a muddy, umbrella-patterned sock.

'What happened to your wellington?'

Nishi sniffed. 'I lost it.'

'How?'

'None of your business.' She wrinkled her nose. 'Why are you covered in . . . in . . . what *is* that?'

'Nothing,' I said quickly. 'I thought you'd been **eaten** by a dinosaur.'

She snorted. 'I can look after myself. Global GUM guidance says that meteorologists should always be ready for unexpected weathers.'

I looked past Nishi to the end of the cave. All I could see was moss and rock.

My inventor's instincts quivered.

'Where's my time machine?'

'Oh, that,' said Nishi. She shrugged. 'It got squashed.'

I goggled at her.

'A dinosaur stepped on it,' she said, looking not even a teensy-tiny bit sorry. 'It got stuck on its foot and off it went.'

'Went where?' I said incredulously.

'Through the trees. I tried following it, but it was too fast, then I lost my wellington. Luckily I found this cave. I've been hiding here ever since.'

I couldn't believe it.

I'd given away my Self-cleaning Specs.

I'd been almost spuzzled by a **Berthasaurus**.

I'd been dino-napped by a **pterodactyl**.

I'd lost my INSTA DE-STICKER SPRAY.

And I'd been **ROBBED** of my first edition *Inventor's Handbook*.

I'd been through all this **HEARTACHE** just so I could get ~~my~~ our time machine back, and my DRONG of a sister had let it get *CRUSHED*.

Had I not been standing in front of her, I would have absolutely started howling there and then.

'Why didn't you stop the dinosaur stepping on it?' I demanded.

'Because I was too busy trying **NOT** to get trampled myself,' she snapped.

'You should have done *SOMETHING.*'

'Like what? Ask it nicely to give it back?'

'That was my chance to win the Young Inventor of the Year contest,' I hissed, my fingers itching to **BOP** her with my **Extend-a-Hand**. 'My chance to prove to the world that I'm a **genius inventor**. The contest is **TOMORROW**.

How am I supposed to win the Brain Trophy without it?'

'You're worrying about **a trophy?**' squawked Nishi in disbelief. 'My GUM exams start tomorrow and I only just saved myself from being *flattened.*' She pointed a grubby finger at the cave entrance. 'It's a forest of teeth out there! Do you understand?

A.

Forest.

Of.

TEETH.'

She stopped and looked at me in sudden realization. 'How did *you* get here anyway? If your time machine was here –' she waved her fingers in the air as if she was trying to process a complex equation – 'and you were there—'

See what I mean? A TOTAL DRONG.

'I came in a Perombulator.'

'A helicopter?'

'A Perombulator. Like my time machine *that got*

squashed, it travels through all of time and space aka the Murkle.'

And I told her the whole story minus a few details (OK – maybe a lot of details, especially the teensy-tiny detail of breaking T.O.O.T. regulations).

It was hard to tell exactly **what** Nishi thought of this story since her face was CAKED in dried mud.

When I'd finished, she took a long, deep breath and said, 'Those Butterfly Ripples aren't my fault. You should have thought of that when you built a time machine.'

I g°ggled at her. After hearing about my adventures through space and time, that's all she could say? It was a miracle we were even related.

'It was the first prototype,' I spat, my voice sizzling with fury. 'And now it's gone. Because of YOU. I told you **NOT** to press that button.'

'And now you've lost Broccoli and this . . . Steven—' said Nishi, pretending not to hear me.

'Secondus,' I snapped.

'– and the Perombulili.'

'Perombulator.'

'And we have to reach them before this star shower or we'll be stranded here?'

A real **genius**, my sister.

'How do we get to them?'

'Climb, Find and Pilot,' I declared irritably.

Nishi stared at me as if I'd gone mad. 'What?'

I cleared my throat. 'Chapter 42 of the *Inventor's Handbook* says that the best inventors always plan in **stages**. Stage One: I climb a tree.'

'A tree?' said Nishi doubtfully.

'Trees are extremely useful thinking and hiding places,' I continued, giving her an *ESHA LASER GLARE*. 'They are **ALSO** very good for seeing things that cannot be seen from the ground. Luckily for *you*, the *Inventor's Handbook* includes tree-climbing as an *important skill* for **inventors**. I am practically an **EXPERT**.

'Stage Two: I use your binoculars to spot the Perombulator. Because **OBVIOUSLY** we can only find it when we know where it is.

'Stage Three: you use your compass to navigate us there. Climb, Find and Pilot.'

Nishi blinked.

'I know – it's a BRILLIANT plan.'

'Brilliant?' she said with a *snort*. 'It's **hopeless!**'

(This is why she is **NOT** an **inventor**.)

I folded my arms across my chest. 'Have you got **anything better?**'

'Well, I . . .' She paused for a **LONG** moment. 'What if we just *wait here* for them to find us?'

I stared at her incredulously. 'And what if they can't get here before the star shower? We'll be **STRANDED.** Is *that* what you want?'

She stuck out her chin. 'I don't want to be stranded **anywhere** with you.'

'That's something we agree on,' I **huffed.**

'But I can't,' said Nishi.

'Can't what?'

'Global Gum Guidance says that meteorologists should be able to navigate in all weathers.' She bit her lip. 'Last time I tried using my compass I failed the **GUM** exams. What if I get it wrong?'

'I thought you'd been practising.'

'Not in a **prehistoric forest,** I haven't! What if we get **lost?**'

'We're lost already,' I reminded her impatiently. 'That's why we need to follow my **genius plan.** So that we can be **found.**'

'And if we find this Seconi, he'll definitely take us home?'

At that moment, I didn't think it was a good idea to tell her about being in trouble with T.O.O.T. Not when I needed her help to get back to the Perombulator before nighttime. Instead, I decided that dealing with a DRONG of a sister was like dealing with **dinosaurs**. Sometimes, it was safer to keep quiet.

Crossing my fingers behind my back, I looked at Nishi and said in my very best serious voice, 'That's exactly what Secondus told me.'

'What about the Butterfly Ripples?' said Nishi. 'You said I need to be stabilized, remember? If I accidentally create any more, we could destroy all of reality! Mum and Dad will be *furious*.'

'Ah.' I grinned. 'Luckily for you, DRONG-BRAIN, you have a **genius sister**.' With a flourish, I pulled out the stabilizing sherbet that I'd taken from the Primary Console.

'What is *that*?' she said.

'Stabilizing sherbet. I was planning to keep it for further investigation.' I stared at it sadly, then handed it to her. 'But considering I'm the FIRST EVER genius

inventor to invent a time machine IN HISTORY AND BEYOND, I'm sure I can figure out ripple-free travel without it.'

(Actually, I wasn't sure if I was the first inventor to crack time travel, but I didn't need to tell Nishi that.)

'Are you sure it's safe?' she asked, staring at it suspiciously.

'Absolutely.' I grinned suddenly, a devilish thought fizzing in my head. 'Just make sure you bite it straight away.'

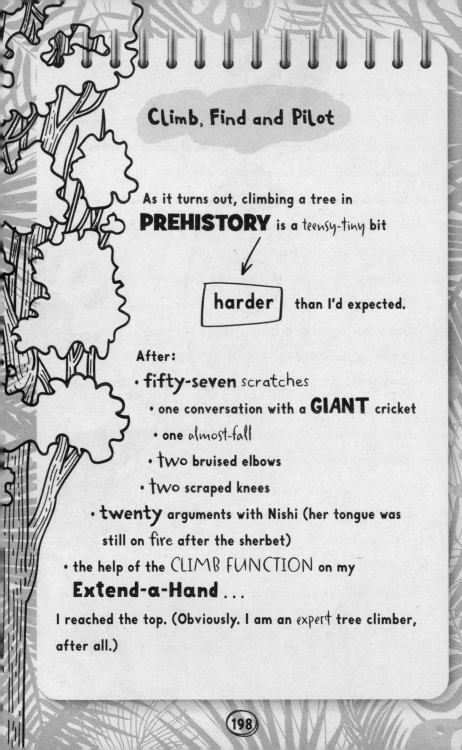

Climb, Find and Pilot

As it turns out, climbing a tree in **PREHISTORY** is a teensy-tiny bit

↓

| harder | than I'd expected.

After:

- **fifty-seven** scratches
  - one conversation with a **GIANT** cricket
  - one almost-fall
  - two bruised elbows
  - two scraped knees
- **twenty** arguments with Nishi (her tongue was still on fire after the sherbet)
- the help of the CLIMB FUNCTION on my **Extend-a-Hand** . . .

I reached the top. (Obviously. I am an expert tree climber, after all.)

On either side of me was an enormous sea of green. The sky looked close enough to touch (almost), the clouds shimmering like silvery-pink fish. In places, the trees suddenly shook, their tops trembling.

Far away, I counted **three** hills at different locations, each one swelling out of the ground like an enormous sock mountain.

Holding the binoculars to my eyes, I squinted at the first. **Nothing.**

Then the second.

No Perombulator.

On the third, I paused and pressed the binoculars closer to my face.

Through the lens of the binoculars, it seemed as if the air were vibrating. Then suddenly – **BAM** – the Perombulator appeared on the hill. Before I could blink, it disappeared. Only a moment later – **BAM** – it reappeared *again*. I squinted through the binoculars, certain I couldn't be seeing it right. There it was again!

One thing was for sure: even from this distance, I could see that the Perombulator was

upside down.

I watched in complete confusion (a very odd feeling for a **genius inventor**) as it kept repeating the same movement. The machine was flickering as if it were trapped inside a fuzzy TV screen. I watched for some moments longer, but it continued disappearing and reappearing, always upside down.

I might not have been an Officer of Time and I absolutely did not own a Perombulator (yet), but I did have **genius inventioning instincts.** And Chapter 23 of the *Inventor's Handbook* said the best inventors always listened to their inventioning instincts no matter what.

At that moment, Reader, mine were

pricklier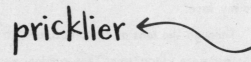

than a grumpy hedgehog.

As I ducked back down the leaves, my brain buzzed with questions.

Why was the Perombulator upside down? **Did** that mean Broccoli and Secondus were upside down too?

Where were the **pterodactyls?** Had they fought them off?

And **WHY** was the Perombulator *flickering*?

It would be such an inconvenience if something had happened to it. In fact, I thought, as I zoomed down the tree, it would be even more of an inconvenience if something had happened to Broccoli. Especially after I'd spent all that time training him.

Good apprentices, *after all*, were like

GOLD
DUST.

'Found it,' I grunted to Nishi as her face came into view. With an expert leap, I hopped down beside her.

She wrinkled her nose. 'You really do **stink.**'

'We need to go that way,' I said, deciding that it was absolutely not a good idea to tell her about the Perombulator.

Nishi popped some gum into her mouth (but did not ask **ME** if I wanted any) and held the compass in front of her.

'South,' she said.

There was a loud screech in the distance.

Nishi hesitated, her compass trembling. **'What about the dinosaurs?** They'll sniff us from miles away.'

'No, they won't.' I looked at my dung-encrusted arms and grinned.

 'I have an idea.'

Jammed

(written mostly by Broccoli)

'W-h-a-t'-s h-a-p-p-e-n-i-n-g?' I cried, my teeth rattling. Archibald's shell was shaking so hard I was afraid it might fly off.

'WARNING,' said the Primary Console. A shrill alarm sounded above my head. 'JAMMED. EVASIVE ACTION RECOMMENDED.'

'O'clocks!' cried Secondus. 'The Academy warned us about this. We're stuck between time zones!' His bowler hat bounced down towards my feet. 'Must've been that last one that did it!'

'JAMMED. EVASIVE ACTION—'

'We're still upside down!' I wailed. 'I thought this wasn't going to take long!' My stomach was churning faster than when I'd eaten that anchovy sandwich at Uncle Roger's.

'TOOT TOOT, officers. We regret to inform you that Officer Weekus Peekus has been guzzled—'

Through the window flashed the pink skies of the Cretaceous Age. Then they were gone and I was looking at a trio of Neanderthals, their faces fierce as they aimed their spears at us. In a moment they'd disappeared and I was watching a stream of time-space particles glittering in the Murkle.

'No change in the Ripple Meter, thank the clocks!' shouted Secondus. A clunk. 'I'm resetting the navigation systems. That'll de-jam us. You might feel a little strange.'

A peculiar floating sensation had taken hold of my body. My arms and legs felt light, heavy, light again, then my head began spinning.

'SEC - ON - DUS!' I shrieked.

Archibald poked his head out of his shell, his worried face whirling before my eyes.

[A note from Esha: I am quite sure that menacing reptile was having the time of his life.]

'My father taught me that trick,' said Secondus, his voice sounding strangely far away. 'Did the same thing when he got jammed in the Crab Nebula—'

But I didn't hear any more.

Because at that moment my head stopped spinning.

And everything went dark.

[A note from Esha: I have since been informed by Secondus that Broccoli fainted. Apparently, it is a side effect of Time Spins that affects 0.01% of people. I have told Broccoli that he should practise the Upside-Down Pose to stop this happening again. This will also help him come up with more GENIUS ideas. A must for any genius inventor's apprentice.]

Swamps and Solidifiers

'I can't believe I listened to you,' moaned Nishi for the HUNDREDTH time. She sniffed her arm. 'I'm never going to wash this off.'

We were still walking through the forest. It was starting to feel like the LONGEST walk of MY. ENTIRE. LIFE. My feet were aching, my sweat was sweating and my Inventor's Hat was so sticky that I was certain I'd need a crowbar to take it off my head. Even worse, I'd been forced to listen to Nishi whining about **dinosaur dung** the whole way.

She stopped suddenly and looked up at the sky with a frown. 'Those look like cumulonimbus clouds.'

I groaned and dug into my pocket, desperately searching for some earplugs – cotton wool – *anything* that would save me from a yawn-boring-yawn lecture on *cloud-spotting*. As I pulled out a few buttons (sadly not suitable for ear-plugging), a leaflet fell down beside my feet. I picked it up, my inventor's instincts tingling with curiosity.

It was the leaflet I'd been given at T.O.O.T.

'Beware the Guzzler,' I murmured, reading the front page.

'Are you listening?' snapped Nishi.

I sighed and shoved the leaflet back into my pocket without looking inside it. Forget Guzzlers. I had a real-life monster to deal with right next to me. *And* I hadn't found any earplugs.

'I *said* that cumulonimbus clouds could mean there's a storm coming.' She tapped her aneroid barometer. 'The needle's moving to CHANGE. Maybe we should take cover. This *is* a different atmos-'

'We don't have time,' I interrupted, stomping ahead of her. Above us, the sky was changing from silvery pink to murky blue. A giant firefly-looking insect buzzed above our heads and landed on a tree branch, its wings glowing. 'It's going to be dark soon.'

She huffed, glaring at her compass. 'If it wasn't for your **stupid** time machine, I'd be in my bedroom learning about air pressures and hygrometers right now. I wouldn't be in the middle of **dinosaur nowhere.**'

'If you hadn't pressed The Big Red Button, you wouldn't have zapped YOURSELF AND MY TIME MACHINE here, and we wouldn't be in the middle of dinosaur—'

I was interrupted by a familiar **THUNDER-RUMBLING ROAR** in the distance.

I froze.

Was it <u>following</u> me?

Nishi grabbed hold of my hand. I stared at the darkening forest and hoped she couldn't feel me trembling. But there were **no** more roars, **no** dinosaur appearing through the trees.

When I was *absolutely certain* we were safe, I pulled away from her (but not too far).

'We need to keep quiet,' I HISSED. 'Or something will hear us.'

'Stop talking, then,' whispered Nishi.

A few minutes later, we came out of the trees on to the edge of a colossal swamp. A pool of **dark sludge** stretched out in front of us, blocking our path. The liquid bubbled and spat. It stank of old, rotten things. The swamp was covered with lily pads. They were HUGE, almost as big as small cars. On either side of the sludge were even more **ENORMOUS** trees with branches that curl-twirled down like long claws.

Nishi scowled at the swamp, chewing frantically. 'We'll have to go round,' she said.

I shook my head. 'I told you already. We don't have time. We have to get back to the Perombulator before the star shower.'

'How else are we going to get across?'
I looked at the lilypads, my brain
SPARKING with the beginnings of a

GENIUS IDEA.

'We can use these. Look.' Slowly, I put one foot on the lily pad nearest to me. It bobbed a little beneath my weight, but stayed where it was. 'It's all a question of surface area and displacement. Chapter 46 of the *Inventor's Handbook*: The Phizztastic—' I took a deep breath and readied myself.

'Esha—' said Nishi, her eyebrows shooting up in warning.

'– Fascinations of Physics,' I finished, leaping on to the lily pad. It rocked for a moment, but, as I'd already guessed, did not sink. I grinned at my DRONG of a sister. 'See? What did I tell you? Easy.'

Nishi pretended not to look impressed as she jumped on to another lily pad. Then she gave me a sly grin. 'Bet you can't get to the other side before me.'

Before I could answer, she leapt ahead with an evil cackle. **'Come on, SLUG!'**

'OI!' I shouted, jumping after her. 'That's CHEATING!'
We must have been about halfway across the swamp

when our contest was **RUDELY** interrupted by a rumble of **THUNDER**.

Nishi stopped and looked up at the sky. 'I knew it!' she cried. She waved her barometer at me. 'What did I tell you? Rain.'

I snorted. 'So what? It's just a little wat—'

Just then, a single bullet of water, the size of a **boulder**, zipped down from above and crashed into the swamp, sinking a lily pad with it. Then came another, smashing through a second.

'*That* isn't rain,' I said, open-mouthed.

'Yes, it is,' snapped Nishi. She pointed at the ugly cloud looming over us. 'And THAT'S a cumulonimbus.'

As if it had heard us, the cloud suddenly opened fire. We vaulted forward as the raindrops zinged down upon us in an **EAR-POPPING thunderous rush**.

'I told you we should have taken cover,' shouted Nishi over the noise.

The water whizzed through the air with breathtaking speed, punching the lily pads into the mud below.

'This isn't rain,' I retorted as I jumped to another pad. 'Rain is never this BIG!'

'WE'RE IN A DIFFERENT ATMOSPHERE,' she yelled.

'EVERYTHING IS BIG HERE.'

I leapt on to another lily pad. At the same moment, a raindrop hit the back of it, flinging me into the air with such force that I flew over the swamp like a tiny insect. My BELOVED Inventor's Hat FELL OFF my head and **vanished** into the mud.

DOOSH!

Nishi's binoculars whizzed out of my hand as I landed – luckily – on to another lily pad. With a sorry *glop-glop*, they also **disappeared** into the swamp.

With a speed that could have won me an Olympic GOLD, I hopped across the remaining lily pads and threw myself on to the bank. Nishi was still moving across the swamp, her face twisted in determination (or irritation– I couldn't be sure).

'This is ALL your fault, Esha!' she yelled.

'ACTUALLY, THIS IS YOUR—'

I stopped as I saw three glowing red spheres moving towards her.

As I watched, the spheres rose above the surface of the mud. Not spheres, I realized. **Eyes.**

The liquid bubbled as a long, thin snout appeared in the water followed by a crooked fin.

'HURRY UP, NISHI!' I shouted.

'What do you think I'm doing?' she snapped.

The creature was moving faster, its fin cutting through the swamp like a knife. Nishi was concentrating so hard on the lily pads that she hadn't even noticed.

UH OH.

'There's something behind you!' I shouted.

'What?'

'BEHIND YOU!'

She glanced back over her shoulder. Like an utter DRONG, she slowed as she spotted it.

'MOVE!' I bellowed.

Nishi leapt forward as if she'd been **SPIZZLED** by an electric current.

Four lily pads to go . . .

three . . .

two . . .

Almost there—

A **massive** spurt of raindrops fired ahead of her, taking out her only path to land.

A long stretch of mud lay between her and the edge of the swamp.

She looked back. The creature was getting closer now. **'Jump, Nishi!'** I cried.

'I can't!' she shouted, her eyes wide with panic. 'It's too far.'

A hungry growl filled the air as the creature approached her. I dug my hand into my Inventor's Kit. There was not a single sliver of a chance I was going to let this swamp-monster digest my DRONG of a sister. Not after I'd gone to all the trouble of listening to the YAWN-BORING-YAWN mechanics of compass navigation.

Scrabbling around, I pulled out four rainbow-coloured bath bombs. At least, they looked like bath bombs. They were, in fact, the second prototype of one of my **genius inventions**: THE SOLIDIFIER.

One by one, I hurled all of them into the swamp. They sank with a **GLUMPTIOUS** fizz-popping sound. A moment later, the mud started to boil. It shot into the air in hissing spurts, fountaining across the rain-soaked swamp with such **FEROCIOUSNESS** that even the creature slowed to **GOGGLE** at the spectacle. Just as suddenly as it had started, the spurting stopped. I watched as the surface of the mud pulled itself tight as if someone were stretching it from either end. A thin film had appeared on top of the swamp, sticky and shiny, like the icing on a chocolate cake.

Nishi looked around in bewilderment.

'Come on, Nishi,' I shouted. The creature was already on the move, its snout breaking easily through the surface of the swamp. 'You have to **RUN** across!'

Nishi hesitated, then she put one foot on the mud. It plunged straight in. She pulled it back and glared at me.

'This is never going to work.'

'I told you to **RUN**,' I shouted. 'If you go too slowly, you'll sink.'

The creature growled, its snout almost within reach of my sister.

I took a deep breath, preparing the biggest *ESHA NINJA BLOW* of my entire life.

'YOU HAVE TO TRUST ME, NISHI!'

I bellowed.

For one heart-sinking moment, I thought she wasn't going to listen.

Then, just as the creature was almost upon her, she leapt off the lily pad.

Her feet skimmed the surface of the swamp like a pond skater as she sprinted across. Raindrops smashed through the semi-solid top like missiles. Nishi dodged past them, the creature still on her tail, then, with a final, almost heroic leap, she FLUNG herself towards me.

But she hadn't leapt **quite far enough!**

With an angry, skin-curling growl, the creature broke through the mud and

opened its jaws,

aiming for Nishi's foot mid-air.

Oh no you don't.

Grabbing hold of Nishi's hand, I yanked her out of the way as – **SNAP** – the creature's jaws clamped down on empty air. We threw ourselves backwards and watched, breathless, as it retreated into the swamp, its red eyes the last to disappear as it sank into the mud.

I sagged to the ground.

Another giant insect fluttered above our heads, glowing against the darkening sky.

'No,' gasped Nishi. She held up a mud-stained object with a crack running across it. Her voice caught in her throat. 'The compass – **it's broken.**'

The Right Way Up
(written mostly by Broccoli)

'Wake up, Insignificant!' shouted Secondus.

Arms shook me. I blinked, Secondus' face spinning round me for a few moments before it wobbled to a stop.

'It worked! We're the right way up!' He waved the SPECIES TRACKER at me. Three green bubbles floated in the cloudy liquid. 'They're alive, thank the clocks! And look—' He jabbed a finger at the two bubbles bobbing beside each other. 'They're together!'

I tried to speak, but my tongue was stuck to the top of my mouth. I peeled myself off the wall and collapsed to the floor. I felt terrible. Even worse than the time I'd been carried away by a fish when Dad took me camping. Archibald crawled out of my pocket and peered up at me, his face wrinkled in concern.

Secondus leapt over me to the door. His hat twitched with excitement. 'Still no movement on the Ripple Meter either. What a stroke of luc— O'clocks!'

'What?' I muttered.

'Those Time Spins took longer than I thought,' said Secondus, his voice dropping.

'Haw moch langer?' I asked, pulling my tongue free with my finger.

Beyond the glow of the Perombulator, the hill was in darkness. I could just about see the forest, the trees looming scarily in the distance. My nose quivered. I hated the dark even more than I hated heights.

'The Academy warned us about zonal time differences!' muttered Secondus, leaping back to the Primary Console. He took off his hat and put it back on again. 'Father would've never made a mistake like that . . .'

The cauldron marked FORECAST hissed and spat. A moment later, a roll of parchment shot out of it. Secondus caught it in mid-air and ripped it open, his eyes darting across the page.

'WARNING: STAR SHOWER IMMINENT,'

he said, his hat wobbling. 'IMMEDIATE DEPARTURE ADVISED.'

'Immediate departure?' I sneezed. 'But we still need to find Esha and Nishi.'

Just then, the Perombulator shook. A fiery shimmer appeared far in the distance above us.

'The star shower,' said

Secondus, a note of fear creeping into his voice. He shoved the SPECIES TRACKER at me. 'Keep an eye on them.'

'This is safe, isn't it?' I asked, holding the device away from me.

The Perombulator **trembled** again, the walls groaning around us.

The sign above the door started to flash.

Archibald and I stared at each other in fright.

'It's affecting the systems already,' said Secondus, hopping towards the Primary Console. The sensors whirred frantically. The screens flickered. The ship's wheel spun.

'WARNING!' said an automated voice. 'STAR SHOWER DETECTED. SYSTEM RISK: HIGH. WARNING!'

The cauldron began to shake.

A fountain of parchment exploded into the air.

'O'clocks,' muttered Secondus. The cauldron rattled back and forth, hissing violently. He stepped backwards.

'Secondus?' I said. 'Is it meant to be making that noi–'

'DUCK!' yelled Secondus, pushing me out of the way.

The cauldron catapulted into the air and smacked against the ceiling before clattering to the ground.

'OW,' I groaned as I wobbled to my feet. Being an inventor's apprentice was definitely a lot more painful than I'd expected.

Secondus was already back at the Primary Console, flicking levers and pressing switches.

'I can't leave the Perombulator like this! If I can just get us steady—'

BANG!

He sprang sideways as a tube next to him shattered. 'Grand clocks,' he gasped, 'not the Ripple Meter! I can't track the ripples without it!'

I looked at the SPECIES TRACKER. If I was reading it correctly, then Esha and Nishi weren't far away.

PING! Another button shot off the Primary Console.

I sniffed and looked at Archibald. He nudged his nose against my palm, then bobbed his head towards the open door. I glanced outside. It really was very dark. But Esha was always telling me that I should be brave. Just like Granny Bertha. I took a deep breath.

'I can do it,' I said, my nose trembling.

A device marked HOOVER switched on with a loud SHOOP noise.

'This is nothing like our practice missions!' cried Secondus. He clutched his hat tightly to stop it being sucked away.

'TOOT TOOT, officers. We regret to inform you that Officer VanHour has been guzzled—'

'I said I can do it,' I said, raising my voice over the noise.

'Do what?' cried Secondus. With his free hand, he pulled another lever and cranked a couple of wheels, his cheeks flapping against the force of the air. With a weary SHOOP, the Hoover switched off.

'I can find Esha and Nishi. I'll use the SPECIES TRACKER.'

'You'll never make it there and back in time,' said Secondus.

'Esha's my friend,' I said with a fierce sniff. 'And Nishi - well - she's Nishi. I won't leave them behind.'

'SYSTEM RISK: HIGH. WARNING!'

'If I could just get this to—' Secondus jabbed a switch.

'Deterrent Mode - Failure.'

A moment later, there was a loud hiss. The Primary Console sparked and flung Secondus back against the wall.

'O'grand clocks,' he groaned, sitting up. 'Those Time Spins used up all the spare power. We don't have enough.'

'Enough for what?' I said.

'A signal,' said Secondus. 'To help them find us.' He took off his hat, his face shiny with panic. 'I'll be the first Secondi to be fired.'

Archibald snickered and looked at my pocket. I stared at him for a moment, then a strange tingling sensation tickled my brain.

[A note from Esha: That is called an idea.]

'You clever tortoise, Archie,' I said, lifting him into the air. 'You're right.' I grinned at Secondus. 'We don't need the Perombulator for a signal. I have just the thing.'

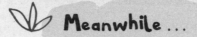 Meanwhile...

'How many times do I have to say it?' I snapped. 'I didn't **mean** to lose the binoculars. They flew out of my hand! And may I remind you that I also lost MY INVENTOR'S HAT!'

Nishi gave me a LASER-BEAM glare that would have made a T-rex tremble. 'You should have been more careful. Those were GUM-certified binoculars.'

'**I SAVED YOUR LIFE,**' I said incredulously. 'You should be thanking me.'

Nishi snorted. 'Thanking you? For what?' She pushed her way through a tangle of overgrown ferns and stomped across the ground. 'My binoculars are gone.' STOMP. 'My compass is broken.' STOMP. STOMP. 'And we're lost.'

'I thought you said south was this way.'

'I said I THINK it's this way,' snapped Nishi. She glanced up at the darkened sky, her face grim. 'We'd better find the Perempoli before this star shower.' STOMP. 'I'm not missing the GUM exam.'

'Pointless? I invented a **TIME MACHINE**.'

'A time machine that got squashed,' sneered Nishi. 'Even if
we make it home, nobody's going to believe you got it to work.'

I opened my mouth to argue, then stopped in sudden
realization. My DRONG of a sister had just given me a
SPINGLY idea. The time machine might have got crushed,
but if I took something back from the Cretaceous Age it
would be evidence. Proof that I had invented a working time
machine. And if I could persuade T.O.O.T. that everything was
Nishi's fault, I might still be able to win the Brain Trophy. All I
had to do was find a souvenir.

Something

unquestionably
DINOSAUR.

'Do you hear that?' whispered Nishi, suddenly grabbing
hold of my arm.

We'd entered a clearing. Moonlight fell through the
trees and made skin-tingling shadows around our feet.
I listened. All I could hear was the sound of our breathing
and the swish of the leaves.

'Hear what?'

'There's something ahead of us,' she WHISPERED.

'You're imagining things.'

'A meteorologist's ears have to be trained to detect any fluctuations in the air,' she said.

'Really? I don't remember you using your ears when I told you NOT to press The Big Red Button.'

'My ears never lie,' said Nishi, ignoring me. 'Just follow me and keep quiet.'

We hadn't gone more than a few steps when she stopped again.

Her mouth fell open.

My heart dropped between my toes.

Ahead of us were **stacks of BONES.** They shone in the moonlight, milky white and smooth. Standing beside them, its giant head resting on its even more giant body, was a **T-REX, asleep.** It was perfectly still, its eyes closed. The only sign that it wasn't FOSSILIZED was its stinky breath, which rippled across the air in hot waves.

Nishi poked me and waved her hands in a gesture that probably meant 'I told you I heard something'. Holding a finger over her nose, she took a step forward, her sock

SQUELCHING across the ground.

The T-rex stirred.

Wriggling her sock off her foot, Nishi TIPTOED past the T-rex, motioning me to follow. I lifted one foot, then another, then stopped suddenly, my **genius inventioning** instincts tingling with a grand feeling of **OPPORTUNITY**.

[A note from Broccoli: Personally, I would have been feeling something quite different.]

What was more **dinosaur** than **a dinosaur BONE?**

It would only take a moment.

I gagged and wobbled as one of the T-rex's **smelly** snores wafted past my face. My foot trembled in the air as I pirouetted towards the nearest pile of bones.

'Esha!' HISSED Nishi.

The moonlight shifted away suddenly, plunging us in total darkness.

'What are you doing?' whispered Nishi fiercely.

Fumbling, I grabbed the bone resting on the very top of the pile.

It was **surprisingly heavy**. The others rattled a little as I lifted it away. The T-rex sighed, its **breath so rotten** I was surprised my eyes didn't shrivel up in their sockets. As I slipped the bone into my pocket, Nishi grabbed hold of my hand and yanked me past the T-rex to the trees on the other side.

'Have you lost your mind?' she snapped. 'We're running out of time to find the Perombulator and you're collecting **BONES?'**

'It's evidence!' I snapped. 'Besides, you don't even know if we're going the right way. I think we need a new plan . . .' I trailed off suddenly. There, above us, rose a SPARKLING SHIMMER in the sky. It was so far away that it looked like a teensy-tiny smudge, but even from this distance I could tell that it was moving towards us.

'The star shower,' I breathed. 'I think it's started.'

Before Nishi could reply, the air EXPLODED.

One moment, everything was still and quiet.

The next, the sky was shaken ALIVE.

A rainbow of colours whizz-bang-popped across the night in front of us.

Blizzards of fiery orange.

Twisting spirals of pink.

Wheels of green that flashed brilliantly blue and red,

before disappearing in a

shrieking squeal of silver.

It was the most stunning spectacle of sound and light I'd ever seen.

'That isn't a star shower,' said Nishi.

I smiled.

'No,' I said. 'That is a Screeching Fizzer Firecracker.'

Something **ROARED** behind us.

My smile vanished.

'And **THAT** is a T-rex waking up.'

Stuck in the Mud

We **RAN** ... hurtling through the trees and leaping over branches towards the Screeching Fizzer Firecracker. It seemed to have lit up the entire forest. Everywhere, we could hear the rumblings and trumblings of dinosaurs waking up as the fireworks continued, growing louder and brighter with each second.

As we KERZOOMED out of the trees, I spotted, at last, the hill ahead of us.

'What *is* that?' panted Nishi.

The Perombulator was now the right way up, but it was shaking quicker than a giraffe on stilts (hint: **VERY FAST**). Suddenly, I saw Broccoli leap out of the door, the back of his trousers smoking purple. A moment later, Secondus darted out and flung a bucket of water over him, before disappearing inside. More purple smoke continued to puff from the front door.

My inventor's instincts tingled to **DANGER MODE**.

Above us, the shimmer of the star shower was growing brighter.

'Hurry up, Nishi!' I yelled, darting forward. 'We're running out of time!'

'What – do – you – think – I'm – DOING?' she huffed as she sprinted beside me.

BANG!

We were almost at the bottom of the hill when the Perombulator's eyescope whizzed into the sky and disappeared from sight.

'Is – it – meant – to – do – that?' panted Nishi.

I was saved from answering by Broccoli who spotted us at that precise moment.

'ESHA!' he shouted. He waved, bouncing in excitement. 'YOU FOUND US! I KNEW YOU WOULD!'

'COURSE I FOUND YOU!' I yelled back. 'HOW COULD I NOT—'

ROAR!

OH NO.

Looking over my shoulder, I saw the **FEARSOME** shape of the **T-REX** charging out of the forest, trees cracking and crumpling in its path.

Coming for us.

'We're never going to make it,' cried Nishi. 'It's too fast!'

The T-rex bellowed so loudly that my ears popped.

'IT'S A T-REX!' cried Broccoli unhelpfully.

I dug my hand into my Inventor's Kit and pulled out a bottle of sparkly sea-blue liquid.

'Super-strong Sticking Glue,' I shouted. 'This should slow it down!'

The T-rex was at the bottom of the hill now. It thundered after us like an oversized tractor, its tiny arms flapping in the air. The space between us was growing smaller and smaller with every wobbly leap.

Above us, the Screeching Fizzer Firecracker continued to make a racket loud enough to be heard in the twenty-first century.

Holding tight to the bottle, I squeezed a trail of glorious stickiness behind us.

The earth shook as the **T-rex** drew nearer. I looked back just in time to see it step down on the line of glistening glue. It pulled to a sudden halt, its entire body swaying unsteadily.

A screen flew out of the Perombulator's doorway, narrowly missing Broccoli, who threw himself flat on the ground.

Secondus charged out, picked it up, then paused when he saw us *and* the T-rex. His hat shot half a mile into the air.

'IT'S A T-REX!' he shouted.

Honestly.

With a **THUNDER-RUMBLING ROAR**, the T-rex yanked its foot upwards, the glue snapping off with a loud crack.

'It needs more binder!' I yelled. 'I knew I should've used more cornflour!'

The Perombulator rose above the ground and crashed back down. Secondus dived out of its way, landing on Broccoli.

The star shower flooded the entire hill with its light.

'FORGET CORNFLOUR!' shouted Nishi. Her face was wild, her hair bouncing like a party of electric eels. 'USE THAT!' She flung out her arm to a hollow pool of mud that we could now see ahead of us. There were patches like it all over the hill, but this one was the biggest, stretching across the ground like an oozing scar.

'NATURAL BINDER!

ROAR!

Behind me, I saw the T-rex's TINY EYES flashing at us, cold and hungry. Each THUMP of its feet sent shakes through my shoes and shudders through my spine.

The Perombulator floated up into the air and whizzed back down with a mighty THUD.

This time, the ground shook so hard that I, Esha Verma, **genius inventor extraordinaire**, TRIPPED.

THE BOTTLE FLEW OUT OF MY HAND.

'Gotcha!' yelled Nishi, catching it behind me (not bad for a DRONG). She seized my hand and yanked me up, shoving me ahead as the T-rex charged towards us, so close that *I could feel its warm breath prickling the back of my neck.*

Trying not to think about its jaws, I focused ahead of me, my legs pumping at TOP SPEED.

'MIGHTY CLOCKS!' yelled Secondus. He grabbed Broccoli and pulled him inside the Perombulator.

Hardly daring to look back, I vaulted over the mud, Nishi a heartbeat behind me. With a battle cry, she yanked off the bottle top and emptied the glue into the mud below.

As we landed on the opposite side, we glanced back to see the T-rex smash through the mud with its left foot. Its head reached down towards us, its teeth moments away—

Suddenly it pulled to an abrupt halt, its right foot dangling in the air like a ballerina.

In front of us, the Perombulator spun violently.

A shrill Broccoli-sounding scream echoed through the door.

The T-rex's arms flapped as it tried to balance itself, its right leg spun, then, with one mighty wobble, it began to topple forward . . .

slowly . . .

slowly . . .

'I CAN'T HOLD IT ANY LONGER!' bellowed Secondus.

'YOU'RE NOT LEAVING US!' hollered Nishi.

With two **enormous leaps**, we flung ourselves inside, Nishi landing with a heavy THUD on top of me as the Perombulator lurched into the air.

DOOSH!

The T-rex crashed to the ground with an **enraged roar**.

'Where's your time machine?' yelled Secondus as he jabbed the Primary Console.

'SMASHED!' I shouted back.

'Smashed?' echoed Broccoli with a squeak.

'Discombobulated grand clocks!' cried Secondus.
He threw a paper bag at Nishi. 'Stabilizing sherbet. Eat it!'

'ESHA GAVE ME ONE ALREADY!' shouted Nishi. 'I'M NOT
HAVING IT AGAIN!'

'How did— oh never mind!' blustered Secondus.
'We have to get out of here!'

The star shower was almost over us now, the sky
illuminated in a fiery dazzle.

'NO TIME FOR A SENSOR CHECK!' he roared.

'WE'RE
ENTERING
THE MURKLE
BLIND!'

Archibald's face lit up with *savage* delight.

The Perombulator trembled furiously, its familiar screeching drowned out by the **THUNDER-RUMBLING ROARS** of the T-rex as it watched us leave, close enough for me to see its eyes, **wild** and **angry**.

'WARNING! WARNING!'

Its tiny arms reached out, its claws scraping against the side of the Perombulator, and then, with a fearsome

RAT-TAT-TATLING, we were gone.

'*WARNING! SYSTEM RESET NEEDED,*' screeched the Perombulator. It whirled with hair-bobbling speed. **'*URGENT ACTION ADVISED. WARNING!*'**

'Mighty grand clocks!' shouted Secondus. He punched buttons with the speed of a rocket-powered rabbit. Screens flashed, lights flickered and a garble of voices echoed over each other as the Perombulator lurched into the Murkle.

'*Monster Guide. Worm. Habitat: wormhole. Existence: confirmed. Danger: moderate.*'

'*TOOT TOOT, officers—*'

'What about the ripples?' I cried. 'The flying sharks?'

'They never became permanent!' shouted Secondus. 'They'll have collapsed now that—'

'What's collapsed?' cried Nishi.

The Primary Console sparked violently. '**THIS ISN'T THE MOMENT FOR QUESTIONS!**' bellowed Secondus.

'I don't feel so good!' squealed Broccoli as he gripped onto the rail. He sneezed. Once. Twice. **THREE TIMES.** Archibald poked his head out of his pocket and **HALOOTED** with laughter.

I smacked against the window with a thud. Through it I could see the outline of a dark hole. A time-space particle floated inside it, shrivelled up like burnt paper and disappeared.

An **alarm** sounded.

'WORMHOLE DETECTED – DANGER – WORMHOLE—'

UH OH.

'W-w-wormhole?' stammered Broccoli.

A thick cloud of smoke was **puffing** out of the Primary Console.

'The systems haven't reset yet!' bellowed Secondus. 'I can't adjust the thrusters!'

(I am absolutely sure that ~~my~~ our time machine would have been *far* less glitchy.)

There was a DRONG-like scream.

'This is the *worst rescue EVER!*' shouted Nishi, whizzing past me. Her arms spun like a windmill, her hands clutching at empty air as she fell to the floor.

'*DOOR LOCK- FAILURE.*'

The Perombulator door flung open.

'*The Guzzler. Habitat: wormhole. Existence: confirmed. Danger: high.*'

'Guzzler?' I shouted.

'G-g-guzzler?' squeaked Broccoli.

'*– wish you safe travels – TOOT TOOT –*'

'*SYSTEM RESET COMPLE—*'

There was a

gigantic WHURMP

as the Perombulator spun ROUND and ROUND, tossing us like fish in a whirlpool – '*WARNING! WORMHOLE DETECTED*' – until it creaked to a sudden, final STOP.

The sign above the door pinged wildly from **ACTIVE** to **STANDBY** and back again, then fizzled out completely. The door flapped, a thick fog twisting beyond it.

Broccoli unstuck himself from the wall and collapsed to the floor.

'Mighty clocks!' shouted Secondus.

'We've fallen inside the wormhole!'

The screens on the Primary Console were blank. The ticking of the Sat-Nav was silent. Secondus took off his hat and put it back on again, his face twisted in alarm. 'The systems won't work here!'

'It's cold,' stuttered Broccoli, his breath forming vapoury puffs in the air.

'I have to take manual control,' babbled Secondus. His hat twitched in panic as he darted to the ship's wheel.

'In my **genius** opinion, your Perombulator has at least TEN design faults,' I began.

'Propellers . . . propellers . . .' continued Secondus. He pulled a series of levers beneath the ship's wheel. With each movement, there was a light clunk. 'Activated. Look for the Murkle's light. We have to find it before—'

TH∪MP!

'What was that?' whispered Nishi. Tiny crystals of ice sparkled on her hair.

TH∪MP!

My inventor's instincts tingled to TROUBLE as we looked through the window.

Worms

On the other side, hovering in the dark fog, was a
SWARM of flying creatures! Each one was long and
skinny with sharp claws and HUGE, leathery wings.
They were almost completely covered in dark wiry hair.
All that could be seen of their faces was a single bloodshot
eyeball, each and every single one focused on us.

'**WORMHOLE WORMS!**' yelled Secondus.

He yanked the ship's wheel, and the Perombulator swung
round with a loud groan. '**SHUT THAT DOOR!**'

With a SUPREME leap, I flung myself towards it.
Unfortunately, Secondus had told us just a little too late.

Screeching loudly, two of the repulsive worms rocketed
inside the Perombulator. One (understandably) knocked
Nishi off her feet, the other darted above our heads with a
gleeful giggling noise.

A speckled yellow tongue **shot** out of its hair and whizzed towards Secondus. Before he could move, the worm snatched up his bowler hat and slid it on to its head. Well, the part of it that *looked* like a head.

'Not my hat!' shouted Secondus. 'GIVE THAT BACK!'

Dancing out of his reach, the worm slipped the hat into its hairy fuzz. **CRUNCH! CRUNCH!**

Its entire hairy body waggled in delight.

'No,' gasped Secondus. He glared at the fuzzball with utter venom. 'That was my *first* T.O.O.T. hat, worm.' With a **furious holler** (and absolutely no warning) he twisted the ship's wheel firmly to the right.

I grabbed hold of the rail.

Broccoli shrieked as he whizzed to the other side of the Perombulator, his hand clutching a fascinated Archibald.

[A note from Broccoli: That was not fascination. That was shock. No tortoise should have to see what we saw on that day.]

The worm spun. Secondus tugged the ship's wheel the other way. Then right again. Then left. But the worm had steadied itself now, its eye fixing on ME. I whipped out my **Extend-a-Hand**, ice splintering off the metal as I pressed the SWAT setting. I'd had enough of foul fuzz-brains wanting to gobble my **genius** self.

'HA!' shouted Nishi as she kicked the second worm out of the door.

'AAAAAAHHHHHH!' I screamed, charging at the bowler-hat-thieving worm. I swung the **Extend-a-Hand** over my head like a baseball bat. With a satisfying **THUMP**, it sent the creature cannonballing towards Nishi, who ducked just in time. The worm sailed outside, performing a pirouette that would have made a prima ballerina puff up with pride. With a shrill giggle, the worm slid out its tongue and FIRED it at Nishi's foot.

'GET IT OFF ME!' she squealed as the worm's tongue curled itself round her remaining wellington and dragged her towards the edge of the doorway.

With BEWILDERING bravery, Broccoli threw himself forward and grabbed Nishi's arm.

'Esha!' he gasped as he slid across the Perombulator. **'Do something!'**

With **genius** quick-thinking, I seized hold of his trouser leg and pushed the HOLD button on the **Extend-a-Hand**, aiming it at the rail. It sprung forward and locked on to it, nearly pulling my arm out of its socket.

The worm let out a vicious giggle and tugged Nishi's STINKING wellington so hard that she rose upwards, pulling us along with her so that we were all hovering in the air.

Outside, the other (fuzz-headed worms) were still
following us, their giggling
growing louder and louder as
they fought to keep up with us.

'They're **attacking us**
from behind!' shouted Secondus, trying to hold the
Perombulator steady.

TOO SCARY TO SHOW

Every second, one of the worms would hurl themselves (or
a tongue, it was hard to be sure) at the Perombulator, and
we would spiral uncontrollably onwards.

Suddenly, the Perombulator dipped sharply.

'O'clocks!' cried Secondus. 'THEY'VE TAKEN OFF A
PROPELLER.'

The Perombulator spun like a snake doing a samba.

It twisted like a tornado on a trampoline.

It hurtled like a horse in a helicopter.

Something fell out of my Inventor's Kit and whizzed
through the door.

'My Grow-your-own-hair Gel!' I cried.

Out fell the spanners, almost taking off Nishi's head as
they KERZOOMED into the fog. These were followed
by:

1. My last reserve chocolate bar.
2. Pens and pencils.
3. Half a ginger biscuit.
4. A clay-sculpting kit.
5. A packet of cress.
6. Two lightbulbs.
7. A plastic mug.
8. Three rolls of bubble wrap.
9. One third of a drainpipe.
10. Knitting needles.
11. The head of a toothbrush.
12. Half a comb.
13. A shaved-off bar of soap.
14. One chopstick.
15. Two dried-out paintbrushes.
16. A roll of tape.
17. The leaflet from T.O.O.T.

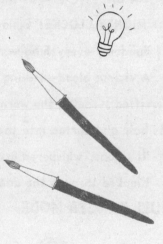

and so on . . . until my entire (sigh) **INVENTOR'S KIT** had disappeared into the dark fog.

'YOU STUPID WORM!' I yelled. 'THAT WAS MONTHS' WORTH OF **GENIUS** COLLECTING!'

The worm's hairy fuzz **trembled with evil.**

'I can't hold on much longer!' cried Nishi.

Pain flashed through my arm as I gripped on to the **Extend-a-Hand**, the entire contraption creaking under the strain.

'It's too strong!' gasped **Broccoli**.

The air SHOOK as the worms closed in on us.

'MIGHTY CLOCKS!' bellowed Secondus. 'They're too fast!'

Suddenly everything went deathly quiet.

A vicious blood-curdling hiss rose out of the fog. With a terrified screech, the worm whipped Nishi's wellington into its hair and darted into the fog, *leaving us <u>not</u> gobbled*.

'It's gone,' whispered Broccoli, sitting up. 'They all have.'

I looked through the doorway, my inventor's instincts on **FULL DANGER MODE.**

Drifting out of the gloom were five shining crescent-moon eyes. Only they weren't shining in a warm, happy way. More like a cold, hungry way. They were attached to long stalks, which were joined to the face of the most

NIGHTMARISH

CREATURE I'D **EVER** SEEN.

It was the width and height of a skyscraper and built like a fish.

It had an enormous pink bulge where its nose probably was, and its face was a dark, scaly green.

Sharp white fangs protruded from its mouth, glistening dangerously in the gloom.

It cut through the swirling mist in quick zigzag movements like an eel.

AND IT WAS HEADED RIGHT FOR US.

'The Guzzler!' gasped Secondus.

'WHAT'S A GUZZLER?' roared Nishi.

'*THAT!*' I shouted.

Broccoli took one look at the creature and exploded into a sneezing fit.

Secondus yanked the ship's wheel, the Perombulator spinning through the fog.

The Guzzler hissed viciously and leaped forward.

Fear clawed at my stomach.

'You're going the wrong way!' yelled Nishi. 'Turn round!'

'I'm trying,' bellowed Secondus, twisting the wheel. His eyes were wide and frightened.

'Too hard!' I shouted. 'Turn us back!'

Archibald smacked his lips, his head bobbing up and down in excitement.

Secondus yanked the wheel the other way, the Perombulator spinning wildly.

'We're too close!' I screamed.

Broccoli sneezed again.

'Grand clocks!' shrieked Secondus, his body frozen in terror. 'The propellers aren't fast enough—'

With a malicious, heart-quivering hiss, the Guzzler opened its mouth, its fangs gleaming as they *clamped down over us*. The ship's wheel spun out of Secondus's hand.

The Perombulator shook violently side to side as we tilted upside d
o
w
n.

UP...

d

o

w

d

o

n...

w

n...

UP...

side...

to...

side...

we tumbled...

and bounced...

and slid... crashing and

falling...

over . . .

and under . . .

each other. . .

until, at last, we came to a

STOP.

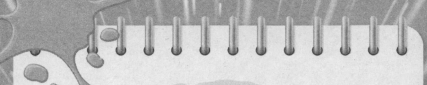

Darkness.

The thickest, most **complete darkness** I'd <u>EVER</u> known.
A loud dripping noise echoed through the gloom and sent
an **ICE-COLD** shiver all over me.

'Broccoli,' I whispered. 'Is that you?'

'No,' he sniffed.

'I **HATE** time travel,' spat Nishi.

With a loud groan, Secondus rolled out from under the
Primary Console. There was a scratching noise as the soft glow
of a lantern flooded through the Perombulator. Wobbling
to his feet, he stumbled to the door and pushed it open.

'Mighty clocks,' he whispered.

Outside, walls as big as mountains stretched down from
a huge arched ceiling and disappeared into a gurgling
pool of **dark liquid**, forming a cavernous pit. Large
droplets of squidgy-looking slime dribbled off the ceiling
and . . . **PLOP** . . . landed in the liquid below.

A bitter smell, like sour milk, hung in the air. Each wall was a pink colour with a pattern of red lines criss-crossing over it. Where they met the liquid, the walls were covered with white seaweed-like floating . . . things.

I stared at these **UNKNOWN** surroundings, every single **inventioning instinct** telling me two important facts:

① We'd been **GUZZLED**.

② This was absolutely more dreadful than being taken to **T.O.O.T.**

'Look,' said Secondus. He waved the lantern at the seaweed-things around the doorway. 'We're stuck.'

Just then, in the distance, came the unmistakeable sound of **GRINDING**.

Broccoli's face turned the colour of a sickly strawberry. 'W-w-what is that?'

At the end of the cavern was an **enormous** opening of fleshy muscle with a circle of razor-sharp structures jutting out from its edges. As we watched, the choppers moved towards the centre then out again – this was the awful **GRINDING** noise!

My breath caught in my throat as a single, fuzzy-haired worm floated towards the choppers. Its wings flapped in panic as it tried to pull itself out of the dark stream of liquid, but with a blood-curdling screech it reached the axe-like teeth – **GREEEEERENNN** – and disappeared.

I gasped.

Not even my *Inventor's Handbook* had prepared me for *that*.

Nishi stumbled backwards.

Broccoli clapped a hand to his mouth.

Secondus shrieked. He shoved me out of the way and darted to the ship's wheel. There was a series of sputtering noises.

'**The propellers!**' he gabbled, his voice raw with PANIC. 'They're GONE. **Every. Single. One.**'

'There has to be another way out!' screamed Nishi.

The walls shook and the liquid whirled. The Perombulator trembled dangerously, quivering in the seaweed strings.

'We're going to be mashed! Minced!' wailed Secondus. 'Father would never have let this happen!' He jabbed feverishly at the Primary Console. It remained still and silent.

'You're an **inventor!**' snapped Nishi, turning on me. 'Invent a way out!'

'**We're in a stomach!**' I shouted. For the second time in my **inventioning career**, I realized that *I didn't know what to do*. Not a single idea sparked through my head, not one FLICKER of inspiration tingled my brain. It was absolutely without a doubt **NUMBER ONE** on my list of **WORST Inventioning Moments.**

'And I don't have my Inventor's Kit or my Inventor's Handbook!'

'You're the one who says inventing is all about making something out of nothing!' yelled Nishi.

'He'd be able to find a way out!' Secondus tore frantically through his clipboard. 'There has to be A PROTOCOL to get these systems going. Ah! *If you find yourself guzzled by the terrifying creature known as the Guzzler, The Office of Time regrets to inform you that there is nothing further that can be done. We thank you for all your work and wish you a speedy and painless digestion. Please consider your service as an officer . . . terminated.'*

TOOT TOOT PROTOCOL

'Is that meant to be *helpful?*' shouted Nishi.

'I want to go home,' sniffed Broccoli.

'There has to be something else!' shrieked Secondus, flicking the pages. 'I can't be the first Secondi to be fired.'

I slumped back against the wall and thought about how awful it was that I, Esha Verma, wouldn't be able to win the **Brain Trophy** just because I'd been RUDELY swallowed.

'I think I'm going to be **sick**,' moaned Broccoli.

I stared at him, the familiar

SPINGLY-TINGLY
beginnings of a spark

suddenly lighting up my brain cells.

'Of course,' I said in sudden realization. 'We're in a *stomach*.' I ran to the doorway. Far above, I could see the Guzzler's throat, the skin gleaming, shiny and wrinkled.

'By Hopper and Edison! That's it!'

'I don't believe it!' cried Secondus. 'There's no other protocol for this!' He sagged back against the Primary Console as if all the air had been sucked out of him. His lip quivered. 'We're going to be **digested**.'

The Perombulator slid a little further down, the **GRINDING** echoing around us.

I pulled out what remained of my Inventor's Kit: a screwdriver, my **Extend-a-Hand**, scissors and a ball of string.

It was the sorriest sight I'd ever seen, but that's why my invention was going to be **EVEN MORE GENIUS** than usual.

'Nobody is being digested,' I said fiercely. 'Broccoli, I'm

going to need that free gift from your magazine. The stoga
– stegara – stegoli–'

'The stegosaurus plate?' said Broccoli. 'Why do you want
that?'

'You'll see. Nish, I need your gum. Secondus –' I shoved
the screwdriver at him– 'forget protocols! If you want to
get out of here, I need the wood from the ship's wheel.
We're going to **invent** ourselves a

Throat
Tickler.'

The Throat Tickler
(Or: Esha Saves the Day)
(obviously)

'Will it work?' asked Broccoli, his eyes sparkling with terror.

'It has to,' I grunted, tying the stegosaurus plate to the top of Secondus's clipboard. 'Remember what the *Inventor's Handbook* says? Inventing is about *making the impossible possible*.'

'Ripping up my own ship—' grunted Secondus as he tore off another piece of wood from the ship's wheel. There was enough sweat dripping off him to fill a small swimming pool. He threw the wood to Broccoli who tied it to the growing pile beside his feet.

'– on my *first mission* –'

The Perombulator dropped a little further along the seaweed things, the GRINDING noise echoing around us.

'– with Minor Insignificants –'

'We're at the edge!' shouted Nishi from the doorway. 'Hurry up!'

'– without protocols –'

'WE'RE GOING AS FAST AS WE CAN!' I shouted, without looking up. My **genius brain** was now in FULL CONCENTRATION MODE.

The Perombulator shook again, my stomach turntabling with the movement.

Forcing thoughts of digesting out of my brain, I worked faster and faster, brain and fingers moving at ROCKET SPEED.

GREEEEEEERRRNNNNNNNN

went the choppers.

With a dreadful **SHLUP**, the Perombulator slid a little further along the seaweed strings.

'We're running out of time!' cried Nishi.

'DONE!' With Broccoli and Secondus clutching the other end, I heaved the top of the **Extend-a-Hand** to the doorway.

'Help me, Nish!'

Together, we aimed it at the Guzzler's throat and pressed the **SUPER-EXTEND** button. With a loud squeal, it

KERZOOOOOOOOOOOOMED

upwards, higher and higher, until it stopped just millimetres away from the Guzzler's gullet.

'Move forward,' I yelled, leaning **dangerously** over the doorway. 'Just a little more. That's it!'

GREEEEEEERRRNNNNNNN!

The stegosaurus plate, which was attached to the very top of the Throat Tickler, touched the Guzzler's throat. The surface shuddered beneath it. I leaned out a little more and moved the Tickler across the Guzzler's gullet.

With each movement, the throat quivered, its surface twitching like a bad eye itch.

'Is it working?' cried Secondus. 'I can't see anything from back here!'

'Again,' I huffed. 'We're not there yet.'

Holding bravely on to the edge of the doorway with my left hand, I tipped out as far as I could.

'How much longer?' gasped Broccoli. 'This – is – *heavy*.'

Archibald made a snickering noise which sounded like 'you are all DOOMED'.

All of a sudden, the stomach walls quivered. I rocked sideways, the Throat Tickler wobbling in my hand.

'Keep it steady!' I shouted over my shoulder. 'I think it's working!'

The stomach walls shook again, more violently this time. The Throat Tickler KERZOOMED across the Guzzler's gullet as we pitched back and forth. Meanwhile, the pool of dark liquid around us was beginning to rise and fall in huge, stinking waves.

'Storm's building!' exclaimed Nishi.

GREEEEEERRRNNNNNNN!

Giant bubbles rose into the air and popped like champagne corks as the liquid continued to churn.

It was moving in a circular motion now, twisting into a whirling whirlpool of stomach juices.

The Perombulator swayed unsteadily like a bucket caught in a storm until, with a heart-squeezing SHLUP, it slithered free of the seaweed strings keeping it in place.

'O'clocks!' shouted Secondus. 'We're loose! Unmoored! Adrift!'

GREEEEEEERRRRNNNNNNN!

Archibald HALOOTED with excitement and made a noise that sounded like 'bet Pa has never had an adventure like this'.

We **plummeted** to the centre of the whirling whirlpool, the Perombulator twisting quicker than a teacup on a fairground ride. I held on tight to the doorway with my left hand, the Throat Tickler jolting about in my right as we

SPI- RAL-LED like the pattern on Archibald's shell,

FASTER and FASTER

the stomach walls

dancing before my e y e s.

We rocketed towards the GRINDERS.

They flashed with MENACE, close enough for us to see their jagged edges, their body-crushing spikes.

'It's not working!' wailed Secondus. 'We're going to be digested! Ground up like a gilly-gally. Pummelled like a primple. Flattened like a flibit!'

'FOCUS, SECONDUS!' I bellowed. No grinders were going to flibit *me*. I pushed the EXTEND button again, the Throat Tickler pushing harder against the Guzzler's gullet.

The stomach walls shook and curved towards us with TERRIFYING speed. The Throat Tickler jerked suddenly in my hand, throwing me off-balance. For a moment, I wobbled dangerously over the SURGING STINKING SINKHOLE, the dark liquid churning hungrily beneath me.

With a thunderous ROAR, Nishi yanked me back inside, her face straining against the weight of the extra-extended Extend-a-Hand.

'THE GRINDERS!' shrieked Broccoli. The spiral of muscle LOOMED before us, the choppers twisting in anticipation.

GREEEEEEERRRNNNNNNN!

A fiery pain shot through my arms as the Throat Tickler danced in my hands.

'KEEP HOLD OF IT!' I yelled.

'It's THE END!' bawled Secondus.

'Goodbye, Father!'

Somebody (probably-definitely Broccoli) sneezed.

The Perombulator lurched towards

the fleshy flap of muscle, the dreadful

GREEEEEEERRRNNNNNNNN echoing

all around us. For a moment, I was absolutely sure

that I saw my short extraordinary life **flash**

before my eyes. Then, all of a sudden, the stomach walls

squeezed inwards, pushing against the Perombulator with

such fierce ferocity that we rose upwards, away from the

grinders.

We swirled and spun, caught in a mighty **STOMACH
STORM.** I lurched backwards, slamming into Nishi. Caught

in the pool of churning liquid, the Throat Tickler **leapt
out of my hands** and plummeted past the doorway.

The hand, my most trusty invention, hovered in the air

momentarily as if waving goodbye, then it was gone, the

ENTIRE extendable contraption PLUNGING into the

Guzzler's digestive depths.

We continued to spin and rise, the Guzzler's gullet

looming closer and closer – until we were flying past it – the liquid forcing us along at such **FEROCIOUS** velocity that all we could do was hold on for dear life as we flew along a narrow passage. Stomach juices sloshed into the Perombulator, soaking us from head to toe.

'It stings!' *squealed* Broccoli.

The door clanged shut as we bounced and rattled along, moving at such **BREAKNECK** speed that it was a wonder our necks *didn't* break. I rolled sideways and downways, Broccoli tumbled from the floor to the ceiling, Archibald bounced around like a bowling ball, Nishi smacked into all of us – still we kept on going until –

'THE WORMHOLE!' shouted Secondus, clinging on to a window. 'WE'RE IN THE WORMHOLE! NO, WAIT. THAT'S LIGHT! I SEE LIGHT!'

And suddenly the endless

tumbling and spinning and twirling

came to a halt.

'Ow,' moaned Broccoli.

I groaned, too bruised to do anything but watch as the

fog outside the window spun into the beautifully brilliant sight of time-space particles. The Perombulator hummed. The Sat-Nav stirred into life, the familiar ticking of the arrows filling the air.

'SYSTEM RESET – COMPLETE.'

The Primary Console crackled. 'TOOT TOOT, officers.'

'O'clocks,' gasped Secondus. 'O mighty grand clocks!'

'Are we still alive?' whispered Nishi.

'Alive?' cried Secondus. 'We're back in the Murkle. The Guzzler puked us right out of the wormhole!'

He hopped about in front of the Primary Console in the strangest dance I had ever seen.

'Oh, wondrous vomitus!' he crowed in glee. 'Beauteous bile! Royal retch! We got out! We escaped! The systems are back online! Wait till my father hears about this! No Secondi has ever escaped a Guzzler before. I'll be the very first. Father will be so proud!'

He kissed the ship's wheel and placed his hand on the Sat-Nav. 'Look lively, Insignificants. We have unfinished business.'

Unfinished Business

The Perombulator shuddered to a halt.

'Here we are,' said Secondus. He straightened his tie, smoothed his hair and leapt to the door. 'Headquarters.'

'Headquarters?' echoed Nishi shrilly. 'I thought we were going home.'

Ah. Maybe I *should* have told her the truth about that.

I looked at my DRONG of a sister (who had an aubergine-coloured bruise on her head), then at Broccoli (who looked as if he were about to cry) and finally at Archibald (who looked bored out of his mind) then at the door.

On the other side was the Headquarters of The Office of Time and definitely-dreadful **punishment**. You, the Reader, are probably thinking that this was the best time for me to remember all my **MIND-BLOWINGLY** brilliant **excuses**.

I took a deep breath.

'It's my fault,' I said. 'It was my idea to invent the time machine. It's my fault that Nishi travelled through time without a permit.'

'Esha, what are you doing?' squeaked Broccoli.

'I'm responsible for all the regulations we've broken,' I continued, my voice wobbling a little. 'Nobody else.' I stepped forward. If there were ever a moment for **The Art of Persuasion** this was it. 'You can take me to Headquarters. Broccoli and Nishi should be allowed home.'

'I'm not leaving you behind,' snapped Nishi.

'Keep quiet,' I hissed. 'You don't know what you're talking about.'

'Yes, I do,' she argued. She put her hands on her hips and glared at me. 'I might not know about time travel or permits, but **I pressed the red button** on that time machine. And if you really think I'm going back home **WITHOUT YOU** then *you're* the biggest DRONG I've ever met.'

'She's right,' said Broccoli, his snot trembling. 'I brought the power cable that powered the time machine. I helped build it. We've **all** broken regulations.'

'And we're all going to Headquarters,' said Nishi.

⟶ 'Together.' ⟵

I looked sideways at my DRONG of a sister then at my snot-nosed apprentice, a lump forming in my throat. For the first time in my inventing life, I, Esha Verma, **genius inventor extraordinaire**, was

 speechless.

[A note from Broccoli: In case you were wondering, this miracle did not last very long.]

Secondus nodded, his eyes twinkling as he looked at each of us. 'This way, then.'

Nishi squeezed my hand as we stepped out.

There, in front of us, beneath a dark, grey sky was a dark, grey building with—

[A note from Broccoli: Ahem.]

OK, OK, I'm joking. That's what I was expecting to see. What really happened was that I stepped into a room which:

1. Was drowning in sock piles.
2. Had a mysterious honey-coloured goop on the carpet.
3. Was missing a worrisome chunk of floor.

Nishi's mouth dropped open. 'The Office of Time looks just like your room, Esha.'

'Don't be an **IGNORAMUS**,' I said. '**This is my room**. I'd recognize those **genius vibes** anywhere.'

Secondus licked the tip of his finger and held it in the air. 'Local time: sixteen-thirty hours.'

'What day is it?' I asked.

'The day we left,' said Secondus.

'The day we left?' I echoed, absolutely certain I couldn't be hearing right. 'But that doesn't make sense. We've been gone for ages.'

'Zonal time differences,' said Secondus. 'We've landed exactly one hour after we left.' He counted on his fingers. 'One hour and five minutes after your sister pressed the button.'

'That's all?' gabbled Nishi.

'But that means —' my **GENIUS BRAIN** whirred in spingly realization — '**we're still on today!**' I grabbed hold of Broccoli, who was blinking at the sock mountains as if they were the most beautiful thing he'd ever seen. 'Did you hear that? **We haven't missed the Young Inventor of the Year contest!**'

'I don't believe it,' whispered Broccoli. 'We're back. We're really back.' He sneezed, then he burst into tears and hugged Archibald (who looked utterly distraught).

'And I haven't missed my GUM exam!' beamed Nishi brightly.

I goggled at her. She must have been the first person in all of history and BEYOND to be happy about having an exam.

'But what about The Office of Time?' I said, turning to Secondus. 'The protocols and regulations?'

He smiled, a strange un-Secondus-like smile. 'You're forgetting that my employment was terminated in the Guzzler's stomach.'

'So?'

'Technically, I don't have to follow protocols and regulations any more.'

'You don't?'

'Not until I report back to Headquarters and get my job back.' His smile widened. 'Besides, your time machine was destroyed in the Cretaceous Age. Hardly any point taking you to Headquarters now that it's gone.'

'And the Butterfly Ripples?'

'Fortunately, the Ripple Meter didn't hit DOOM, so

those ripples never became permanent.'

'So we don't need to worry about flying sharks?' whimpered Broccoli.

'No,' said Secondus.

'Or psychic rabbits?'

'Thank the clocks, no. Temporary ripples collapse once their source is stabilized and removed from the time zone, remember? If the meter had reached **DOOM**, they would have become irreversible and destroyed all of reality, of course. It's all a matter of **Ripple mechanics.**'

I blinked. OK, so I might not have understood everything that Secondus had just said, but I'd heard enough.

'So really what you're saying is I saved all of reality?' I said smugly.

'I don't see how—' began Secondus.

'I was the one who gave Nishi that stabilizing sherbet, which meant she didn't create more ripples so the Ripple Meter didn't hit **DOOM.**'

Secondus hesitated. 'Well, I suppose that is – possibly – perhaps – one way of looking at it,' he said.

(I'm sure he meant it was the only way.)

'And you're really letting us go?' said Broccoli. He sniffed, his eyes and nose leaking faster than a block of wet cheese.

'On one condition,' said Secondus. He pulled out a tiny scroll from his pocket. 'You all have to sign an agreement promising **not** to build any time-travel devices for the rest of your life. Or you will be punished with immediate and lifelong imprisonment.'

I goggled at him. 'For the rest of – but that's – you said you don't have to follow regulations any more.'

'Technically,' he pointed out. 'Practically, I can't let you invent another time machine. Not when you could create enough ripples to destroy all of reality as we know it.'

'But I've already thought of ten different ways to improve the first prototype – including a Ripple Meter! All I need is the recipe for stabilizing sherbets—'

Secondus held the scroll out towards me. 'I'm not asking.'

'Give it here,' said Nishi. She scribbled her name across the parchment. 'I NEVER want to travel in time ever again.'

'She's right,' said Broccoli before I could protest any further. To my utter bewilderment, he added his name, then he held the scroll out to me. 'We've had enough time travel to last us the past, present and future. Isn't that right, Esha?'

I glowered at him. 'This could win us the Brain Trophy.'

'We can invent something else,' said Broccoli. 'Something safer and less criminal. What do you say, Archie?'

The tortoise made a noise of disgust.

'Or I can change my mind about taking you to Head-quarters,' said Secondus. 'In which case, your parents would find out exactly when you've—'

'My parents?' I interrupted, my **genius inventing instincts** trembling in warning.

Being **banned** from inventing another time machine was one thing.

Being **banned** from inventing FOR ALL ETERNITY was quite another.

'Actually, I think Broccoli's right,' I declared, hurriedly signing my name. 'We don't need a time machine to win the Brain Trophy. I am a **genius inventor extraordinaire** and Broccoli is a **genius inventor's** apprentice. We can think of lots more exciting and important things to invent.'

Nishi snorted.

Secondus tucked the scroll back into his pocket and held out his hand towards me.

'Esha Verma, **genius inventor extraordinaire**,' he said, 'if it wasn't for you, I wouldn't have encountered a Guzzler and survived. And without protocols, no less.' His eyes shone with a new confidence. 'Not even my father's done that. Who knows? Maybe I can teach him a thing or two myself.'

I grinned and shook his hand. 'Secondus Secondi, New Officer of Time. It has been an honour.'

One by one, he shook the hands (and claw) of the others. 'Broccoli. Nishi. Reptile.'

I eyed his hatless head. 'In fact, the first thing I'll be rebuilding is my Inventor's Thinking Hat. I could make you one too, if you like. FREE OF CHARGE.'

'There's really no—' said Secondus.

'Chapter 34 of the *Inventor's Handbook* says that **the best inventors share their genius inventions with the world**,' I interrupted. 'I could make one for your father too. I can guarantee it'll be better than a **POOT** one.'

Secondus stepped backwards, shaking his head. 'O'clocks, I don't think he would like that.'

'Or a bottle of SUPER-STRONG STICKING GLUE! I haven't perfected it yet, of course, but it won't take me lon—'

Another step back. 'That really won't be—'

'And you should absolutely take a box of **Dizzying Doughnuts!**'

'In case you meet another Berthasaurus,' added Broccoli.

'I'll think about it,' said Secondus. 'Now, I really must be going,' he continued, darting into the Perombulator. 'I have to get a few things repaired before my next mission.

TOOT TOOT, Insignificants!'

'You haven't told us how to get in touch with you!' I shouted as he shut the door behind him. 'I have lots more exciting and important inventions to share!'

A few moments later, the Perombulator began to vibrate, the air shuddering around it. Then there was a small p°p and it was gone, leaving a faint smell of strawberries.

'I should've asked him if he's been to the future!' exclaimed Nishi. 'He might know if I pass my GUM exams.' Her eyes widened as she suddenly caught sight of her muddy socks. 'As for you, Esha Verma, you owe me another pair of wellingtons.'

I snorted. 'You lost those yourself.'

'And a new compass.' She ticked the items off on her fingers. 'And binoculars.'

'Those weren't my fault.'

'And you almost had us eaten by a T-rex.' She looked at me with a DEVILISH smirk. 'Just wait till I tell Mum and Dad. You're going to be in 𝒮☺ much trouble.' With a triumphant toss of her hair, she marched out of my room.

'Mum and Dad will never believe you!' I shouted after her.

'But they'll believe the hole,' she yelled back.

I looked at the hole in the floor and sighed. It was going

to take all of my **Art of Persuasion** to explain that one.

'Just when I'd started to think she wasn't such a DRONG,' I muttered under my breath.

'Wait till I tell **Granny Bertha** I saw a real **Berthasaurus**,' said Broccoli. He lifted Archibald to his face and looked him in the eye. 'Maybe we can be as brave as her one day.'

The tortoise snickered rudely.

I took out my **dinosaur bone** and put it on my bedside table next to the spot I had saved for the Brain Trophy.

Broccoli took one look at it and sneezed.

'What is that?' he sniffed.

'My souvenir from the Cretaceous Age. A **dinosaur bone**.'

'It looks like an egg.' ←

'Don't be absurd, Broccoli. I may not be a pele-crusty-ontologist like you, but I know the difference between a dinosaur bone and a dinosaur egg.'

Archibald inspected the bone with one beady eye and began HALOOTING with laughter, his entire shell trembling.

'It really *does* look like an egg,' said Broccoli. 'Where exactly did you get it from?'

'I found it in the forest,' I said. Probably best **not** to tell him that I'd taken it from a **sleeping T-rex**. 'Now we really have more important things to be thinking about. The Young Inventor of the Year contest is TOMORROW. As we no longer have a time machine, we need to decide what we're entering. *I'm* sure the **dinosaur bone** could win us the Brain Trophy. After all, it's

absolute PROOF

that we inventioned a working time machine. What do you think?'

Broccoli blinked, his eyes wide and watery. **'You're asking me?'**

'You're my apprentice, aren't you? And the best **genius inventors** *always* consult their apprentices.'

'They do?'

'Don't look so surprised, Broccoli. I can't be expected to do the **genius** thinking ALL the time, can I?'

He hesitated. 'Well – I'm not entirely sure if that's the best – what I mean is – what if we enter the Super-strong Sticking Glue instead?'

'Squashed by a T-rex.'

'Or the Grow-your-own-Hair Gel?'

'Lost in a wormhole – honestly, Broccoli, you really need to pay *attention* if you want to become an **inventor** like me.'

Archibald rolled his eyes.

My stomach gurgled. 'I don't know about you, but I'm starving. We're not going to be able to make any **genius** decisions on an empty stomach. Pizza?'

Broccoli eyed the bone suspiciously a moment longer, sneezed again, then he nodded. 'Pizza.'

And that, dear Reader, is **THE END.**

(Sort of. *Not really.*)

Read on for more fun and activities trialled and tested by Esha and Broccoli

Shell-o Pa,

I hope you are enjoying the Amazon. Myself and the HUMANS have now returned from our travels in space and time. I was lucky enough to visit our ancestors, the dinosaurs.

Unfortunately, I was unable to speak to any of them because the HUMANS kept interfering. Every time I approached a dinosaur to introduce myself, the DRIPPY-HUMAN-PET got in my way. Sadly, I didn't even manage to grab a shellfie with my hero, Big T. I have told the DRIPPY-HUMAN-PET that I can look after myself, but he has yet to learn the complexities of Tortoish.

On a happier claw, I did have the good fortune to encounter wormhole worms. I am sure we would have found much to talk about. Alas, the DRIPPY-HUMAN-PET once again stopped me from finding out more about these fascinating beings.

My favourite part of our too-short adventure was being digested by a Guzzler. I tried to snap a shellfie to capture this

thrilling moment. Unfortunately, the HUMANS forced the Guzzler
to eject us before I had the chance. To my extreme annoyance, we
returned from our travels far too soon. I made my displeasure known
to the DRIPPY-HUMAN-PET but he did not appear to notice. I hope you
are having more excitement in the Amazon.

Until next time,

 Archibald

P.S. The ANNOYING-SHE-HUMAN believes she has brought back a
dinosaur bone. She is quite wrong. I wonder what will happen when
the MA-AND-PA-HUMANS discover it is a baby T. I, for one, cannot
wait.

P.P.S. If you have any tips on communicating
with your HUMAN-PET, please let me know.

Create your own <u>Inventory</u>

Thought you were finished with ~~my~~ our first story? Think again!

I, Esha Verma, and my apprentice, Broccoli, challenge you to list your top 3 favourite inventions we used in this adventure to create your very own **inventory**.

For each invention, include its name and draw a picture of it. Broccoli also thinks it would be helpful if you can think of any improvements.

I have reminded him that ~~my~~ our inventions are absolute **genius** and do not need improving AT ALL, but if you do think of any (unlikely) please ~~keep them to yourself~~ add them below.

INVENTION 1   IMPROVEMENTS:

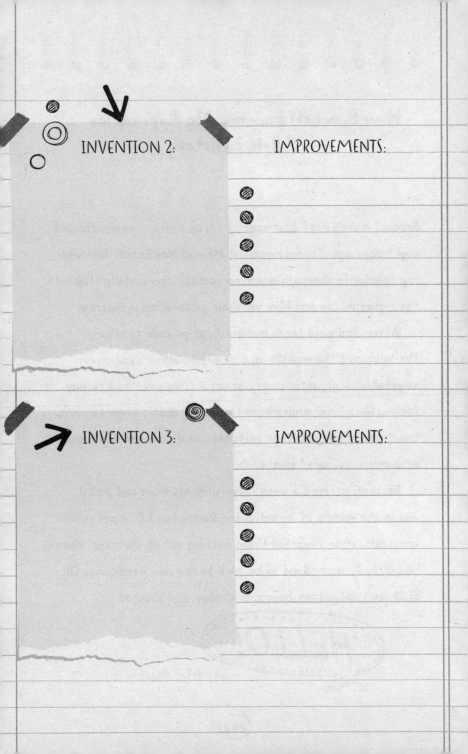

INVENTION 2:

IMPROVEMENTS:

INVENTION 3:

IMPROVEMENTS:

How Broccoli Became My Apprentice...
A Brief History

Broccoli moved next door exactly three years, five months and eight days ago. The last owners, Mr and Mrs Beesal, left when my Bubbler (a shampoo-powered rocket) accidentally flew into their greenhouse and blew up their prize-winning marrow.

After Dad paid them hundreds of pounds to clear the bubbles ('the most' – big angry snort – 'expensive vegetable' – gigantic angry snort – 'I've ever had to pay for' – rhino-level-angry snort – 'and I didn't even eat it'), the Beesal's packed their suitcases and drove off in a puff of marrow-coloured smoke.

Broccoli arrived a week later with his mum and dad. I was in the middle of inventioning Rudolphus 1.0, a pet robot armadillo, when I spotted them getting out of their car. Mum had already warned me to be nice to the new neighbours **OR ELSE**, so I opened my bedroom window and shouted

'HELLO!' in my friendliest voice.

The boy looked at me and sneezed so fiercely that the mysterious box he was holding flew high into the air, sending a green thing whizzing out of it. The even more mysterious green thing landed on my roof with a small **CLUNK**.

[A note from Broccoli: I didn't mean to sneeze so hard. Esha forgot to mention that she was holding a torch gun and wearing her Ultimate Protector helmet when she opened the window. I was **TERRIFIED!**]

'Archibald!' wailed the boy as he gawped at the roof with a THIS-IS-BAD look.

I leaned out of the window to see who he was talking to: it was a tortoise. Lots of shouting and questions later, I'd invented the first prototype of the **Extend-a-Hand** and used it to rescue Archibald from **SPLAT**: becoming a tortoise tortilla. Broccoli was so grateful that he promised to become my apprentice **forever**. Even when I refused, Broccoli followed me around until I finally agreed to keep him as my apprentice.

[A note from Broccoli: This isn't exactly how I remember it happening.]

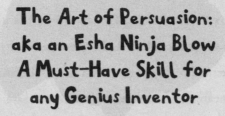

The Art of Persuasion: aka an Esha Ninja Blow A Must-Have Skill for any Genius Inventor

As a genius inventor extraordinaire, you will, no doubt, face moments in your life when your genius ideas will be met with resistance by less-genius people. But do not sob or despair! Like all genius inventors, you too will be able to overcome any such obstacles by mastering The Art of Persuasion.

Especially Mum and Dad and DRONGS AKA Nishi

    A word of warning: becoming an expert in The Art of Persuasion requires training and hours of hard work. But DO NOT GIVE UP. With practice and persistence, you will succeed.

1. The Art of Persuasion is nothing less than going into battle. Preparation is key. Only proceed when you are completely ready.

2. Know exactly what you want before you begin. This is very important. If you are not sure about what you want, it is extremely likely that you will be talked out of it.

Parents are good at this!

3. Timing is everything. ←

Absolutely do NOT bother when Mum and Dad are watching football/ paying bills

See above note on paying bills →

4. Never talk about how much something is going to cost. Ever.

5. Do not accept a Maybe. Maybe is parent-speak for No.

6. If your opponent is proving difficult, try the 'TRADE TACTIC' AKA BARGAIN & BARTER. In order to use this tactic successfully you will need to know your opponent. Super-stealth may be required to collect information (see Chapter 50 for more on this skill).

Dad Likes; football, Extreme Sudoku, samosas, naps
Dislikes: hoovering, marrows, holes in the roof

Nishi Likes: weather, being a DRONG, gum
Dislikes: robot pets, time travel, inventioning

Mum Likes: football, coffee, fluffy slippers, talking on the phone
Dislikes: mess, smelly socks, being interrupted on the phone

General advice: offering to help with housework is proven to work well on parents.

7. If the above does not work, try the 'DOUBLE PRESSURE' tactic. Find someone who can boss your opponent around.

Aunty sha - ??

8. Alternatively, try the 'FLATTERY TACTIC'. Use with caution. This usually only works once before raising suspicion.

Only works on Dad

9. Go back to Number 1 and repeat.

10. If repeating does not work, accept surrender. The best persuaders know that when all else fails, you can try again another day.

A Disclaimer to (less-genius person) e.g. parents, DRONGS, teachers etc. (To be signed BEFORE you begin your very important genius inventions)

This disclaimer hereby forewarns [less-genius person].

I, ... am a GENIUS INVENTOR EXTRAORDINAIRE and I cannot accept any responsibility for any explosions, smoke, weird smells, holes in walls/roofs, other accidents that may arise as a result of my inventing.

Complaints dealing with such inventing matters will be returned unopened. I thank you for your understanding now, then and in the future.

Signed:

Date:

Build your own Dinosaur Mask
(trialled and tested by Esha and Broccoli)

Uses: for scaring DRONGS

What you'll need: paper plate, coloured paint, paintbrush, scissors, glue, coloured card, cotton wool, hole punch, elastic, felt, buttons

A note from Broccoli: (Ask an adult) to help with all the cutting.

① Paint a paper plate with purple paint (or any colour you'd like for your absolutely **TERRIFYING** dinosaur) and leave to dry.

② Once it's dry, cut the plate in half.

③ Use scissors to cut around the edge of one half (this will be your SUPER SCARY mask). You can cut a spiky line or a wavy line depending on what face shape you'd like for your dinosaur.

④ Cut out two eyeholes.

Hint: make them big enough to see through or you will end up crashing into things. You do **NOT** want this to happen when you're trying to scare a DRONG.

⑤ Use coloured card, felt, buttons and your **genius** imagination to decorate your mask (my favourite part). **Hint**: You can cut out dinosaur horns from the card and glue these to the top of the mask (horns are especially useful for poking DRONGS).

Another note from Broccoli: If you want to make a Berthasaurus mask, you can cut a triangle from orange card and stick it between the eyeholes to make its beak. You can also glue cotton wool on its face to give the appearance of fur!

⑥ Once your mask is ready, use a hole punch to make a hole on either side of the mask.

⑦ Loop the elastic through the holes. Make sure it's **big** enough to fit around your head! Tie the elastic with a knot to make sure it doesn't fall off. You also do **NOT** want this to happen when you're trying to scare a DRONG.

⑧ Use your **ROARSOME** mask to scare any and all DRONGS.

P.S. If your dinosaur mask does not scare to your satisfaction, that is absolutely **NOT** ~~my~~ our fault.

Build your own Noisemaker
(trialled and tested by Esha and Broccoli)

Uses: for distracting nosy parents

What you'll need: kitchen roll tube, baking paper, elastic bands, dry rice, dry beans, beads, buttons, paintbrush, paint, scissors, sticky tape, bells

1. Paint a kitchen roll tube and leave to dry.

2. Cut a piece of baking paper into a large circle. Use this to cover one end of the tube. Secure the paper over the tube with an elastic band.

   Hint: Make sure the elastic band is tight over the tube. You do **NOT** want your noisemaker to fall apart when you are trying to distract a NOSY PARENT.

3. Fill the tube with your important noisemaking equipment! This can include dry rice, beads, dry beans, buttons etc.

   Hint: get permission before raiding the kitchen cupboards.

Another Important Hint: Absolutely **do NOT** use wet rice or wet beans. These will make your noisemaker soggy.

4. Once your noisemaker is a quarter full, cover the top end with more baking paper and another elastic band. You can also tape some bells to the outside of the tube to make it even noisier!

5. To distract any nosy parents:

Shake away!

P.S. † We will absolutely **not** be held responsible for any consequences that may result from any noisemaking activity.

Acknowledgements

This book has been a whirlwind of an adventure and I'm extremely grateful to have shared the journey with a TEAM EXTRAORDINAIRE.

Thank you to my brilliant agent, Lauren Gardner, for being with me every step of the way and for steering us through the ups, downs and upside-downs!

Thanks to the WONDERFUL folk at Macmillan for their incredible work and enthusiasm for this book. Special thanks to Rachel Petty who started the book on its way and Samantha Smith for getting it onto the shelves at Perombulatory speed. Huge thanks also to Suzanne Cooper for her amazing book design. I'm also very grateful to Marcus Rashford and Magic Breakfast for the opportunity to share this book with as many readers as possible.

A massive thank you to my fabulous editor, Simran Kaur Sandhu, for all her genius ideas, brain-sparking discussions and faith in this story. This book is so much better because of you.

Thanks also to Allen Fatimaharan for his superb illustrations.

To all my colleagues in CfA, thank you for all your support.

To Afshan, Jasmine, Priyanka and Henna, thanks for always being there for me and for all the laughs along the way.

Finally, an enormous thank you to all my family, near and far, for all your encouragement and belief. I couldn't have done it without you.

About the Author

Pooja Puri is an ~~expert daydreamer~~ inventor of stories. Her debut novel *The Jungle* was published by Black & White's YA imprint, Ink Road, in 2017. *The Jungle* was subsequently nominated for the 2018 CILIP Carnegie Medal. *A Dinosaur Ate My Sister* is her first middle grade novel. You can find her on Twitter @PoojaPuriWrites.

Here are 6 important things to know about her:

1. She likes words.
2. She also likes doughnuts (not exploding ones).
3. Her TOP 3 inventions are: the telephone, the ice-cream cone and glasses.
4. *Jurassic Park* is one of her favourite movies.
5. Her TOP 3 dinosaurs are: the T-Rex, the Brachiosaurus and the Stegosaurus.
6. When Pooja is not inventing stories, she is working on a time machine. It is not ready. Yet . . .

magic breakfast
fuel for learning

You know what happens when a car runs out of fuel or battery power don't you – it just stops! Well, it's pretty much the same for people. When we don't have enough food or drink inside us, we don't have the energy we need to be able to do all the things we want and need to do in a day, like playing with friends, learning maths, or reading a favourite book. It is also really important that the food we eat is healthy, not too full of sugar, and gives us energy that will last the whole day.

Eating breakfast is particularly important as it will probably have been a long time since our last meal, so there won't be a lot of energy left in our bodies to help us focus. Magic Breakfast is a charity that works with lots of schools in England and Scotland to help them make sure all their pupils eat a healthy breakfast, so they are full of energy for the morning ahead.

Magic Breakfast is pleased to have joined Marcus Rashford and Macmillan Children's Books to ensure thousands of schoolchildren from its partner schools receive books from Marcus Rashford's Book Club. Together we aim to encourage reading for pleasure amongst children, especially those who may not have their own books at home.

To learn more about Magic Breakfast you can visit their website: **www.magicbreakfast.com** and remember, always have breakfast at home or at school if you can.

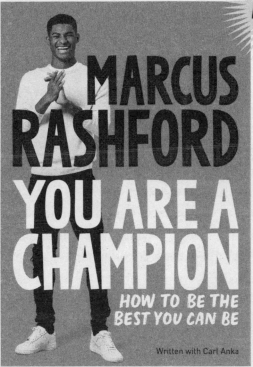

Written with Carl Anka

'It's hard to know what is possible until you start. You have to be able to dream big and be prepared to work towards your dreams. I've achieved a lot so far, but it didn't come in one go; big things rarely happen overnight, and good things rarely happen as if by magic . . .'

Marcus Rashford is famous worldwide for his skills both on-and-off the pitch – but before he was a Manchester United and England footballer, and long before he started his inspiring campaign to end child food poverty, he was just an average kid from Wythenshawe, South Manchester. Now, Marcus Rashford MBE wants to show YOU how to achieve your dreams, in this positive and inspiring guide for life.